A Boat Named Death

Other books by Jack M. Bickham

THE PADRE MUST DIE

THE WAR ON CHARITY ROSS

TARGET: CHARITY ROSS

DECKER'S CAMPAIGN

THE APPLE DUMPLING GANG

JILLY'S CANAL

DOPEY DAN

KATIE, KELLY AND HECK

BAKER'S HAWK

A Boat Named Death

JACK M. BICKHAM

DOUBLEDAY & COMPANY, INC.
GARDEN CITY, NEW YORK
1975

All the characters in this book are fictitious, and any resemblance to actual persons, living or dead, is purely coincidental.

Library of Congress Cataloging in Publication Data

Bickham, Jack M.
A boat named Death.

I. Title.
PZ4.B584Bo [PS3552.13] 813'.5'4
ISBN 0-385-05161-1
Library of Congress Catalog Card Number 74-31512

First Edition

Printed in the United States of America

A Boat Named Death

ONE

Late in the fall, after it was already very cold and the elk had moved down to the lower slopes, the other man came and John Riley Shed killed him.

The other man was not much more than a boy, and very cheerful. He suspected nothing and talked a lot about how the mountains would kill you if they could, which showed he was a fool: the mountains were simply there, and if you knew your business they could not harm you; men were the ones who would kill you, and could never be trusted.

The boy had a new rifle and several boxes of ammunition, so Shed broke his skull open with a rock, dropped him off a cliff, and took his things.

The winter was very bad. Heavy storms followed one another, the wind hurling snow with a force that could cut the skin. Trees broke off, and even the best-protected springs froze solid. Many animals died and it seemed endless. Shed hunkered in his cave with his meat and his fire, going out only now and then to look at the screaming white world for a few moments. Once, on a very still, brilliant day, with the air so cold it froze inside his nostrils and hurt like little knives, he found a gaunt doe struggling in deep snow. He killed it and took it back with him, eating the liver and heart raw and still warm with life, and dressing out the rest. This kill, like the killing of the boy, represented good luck and added comfort. One meant no more than the other.

Shed judged the passing of time only vaguely, by the accumulation of his excrement in the back of the cave. He did not think very much. Once, he had come upon a grizzly in a winter cave, and the great bear had at first resembled a heap of piled furs, scarcely moving, enormous in the enclosed space. Warned by some mechanism that no one could ever understand, the grizzly had stirred then and opened its eyes and gave a slow, coughing snort that sent Shed out of there in a hurry. Shed sometimes remembered the bear during his own long winters. They were alike, he and the grizzly.

Shed's hair grew long in the cave, hanging down his back. Sometimes chunks of meat stuck in his beard and he cut them out. As usually happened, he became infested with vermin, small insects with six legs and horny brown shells on their backs. They were not much bother, but sometimes he spent hours rooting them out of crevices in his body and cracking them between the fingernails of his thumb and index finger. They always had a lot of blood in them, and made a little red spurt when they broke open.

One day, after a long time, the clouds opened for a few hours and the new snow that fell was wet, and glistened in the patchy sunlight. Shed stirred himself to take a walk. He went stiffly down the rocky slope from the cave and through the bitter shade of some frozen birches and out onto a little promontory where the view went out for miles and miles, across rolling white, with pencil-slash trees everywhere, to a jagged horizon.

Shed sniffed the air. This told him things.

There were deer nearby. It would snow again tonight, but not heavily. The spring melt was coming. There was a panther somewhere around.

There was also something else: a sense or premonition of some kind of danger.

Puzzled by this impression, Shed tried to understand it better. He could not. But it was definite. Something in the air or the ground was wrong, somehow. It was still far away, this threat to him, but it was approaching. Warnings stirred in the marrow of his bones.

The danger had to be men. There had never been other men in this country this early in the year, but it was possible. Still, if there were men, they had to be very far off, because he could not detect any physical traces of them, and most men could not walk through a wood without scarring it in a dozen ways by their very presence.

He decided to wait, and went back to his cave. In the night the snow fell gently, and in the morning the sun was brilliant, and warmer. He went out again and found a place on high rocks where the sun's heat had caused a slight melting. A little patch of wet black earth showed through the snow, and a hundred tiny flowers, their stems the size of an eyelash, poked up vivid blue petals. But the feeling of danger was stronger, like an itch in his pores. He could not deny it any longer.

It was time to move.

He carried a canvas bucket of water from his spring to his cave. He removed all his clothing and washed himself, then washed the clothes. With nightfall he laid the clothes outside the cave, and in the morning they were frozen stiff as planks. Shivering from a night only in his robes, he thawed the clothing over his fire and put it back on, steamy and still moist. The washing and freezing had killed almost all the bugs. Using his hunting knife, he cut his hair back to the collar and hacked off most of his beard.

There was a light, powdery snow in the air, but he could not delay. He left the cave and struck out northwest. This was high country, but his destination was higher. If the trapping was good this summer, he might be able to find a place where it would be safe to go and try to sell the pelts. If not, he could find a settler's cabin somewhere and take what he needed and leave the pelts in exchange.

Shed did not like leaving the cave early. The sense of danger forced him. At any rate, he could not stay around here during the softer months. Other men came, like the last one, and you just could not kill everybody.

The mountains, blinding white against the brilliant blue sky, made for hazardous travel. But Shed maintained a strong pace, a big man, gaunt, bushy-haired, dressed in self-made leathers, two bulky packs slung over his back, seldom taking a faulty step as he trekked the way he had gone other years, after other winters, alone.

Four days later, he came to the house.

It had no right to be there.

Shed had been moving through a long, jagged vee between two mountain ridges. It was a geometry world of shale and fallen rock and slashed-up dirt. More than a thousand feet above, black patches of scrub pine marked a leveling off before the rocks piled even higher against the porcelain sky. Below were brush and tumbled rock and a steeply angled drop-off to a narrow river that gushed a tormented path to the south. Along Shed's path was another stream, very narrow but deep, boiling along like a rock-walled ditch suddenly opened to flood. Warmer weather had come fast and the world was made up of melting snowbanks, dripping outcroppings of heavy ice, rivulets, mud, glistening slag, tiny waterfalls, the startling warmth of the sun in cold air, and the cool wet odors of rebirth. The little creek at Shed's feet carried pellmell chunks of broken ice.

Stepping over the ditch, he'd glanced upward, the way he was heading, at an uptilted shale slope running crazily from low left to high right. About two hundred yards up, there it was.

He was totally surprised.

It still looked new, the sides of the timbers black with moisture but the ends and chinks still yellow and fresh. It was a small, square cabin with a roof that had not been given enough slant, with the result that snow was piled on it about three feet deep. There were a door and a window and even a little porch and some steps. Nearby was a lean-to shed, but no sign of animals. Slightly downhill, the spring melt was tearing to pieces a sharply angled area that evidently had been turned over last fall for a garden site.

A wisp of smoke issued from the tin chimney pipe of the house, making a pale question mark against the sky.

Shed watched, testing the scene with every sense and pore. Deep within him, thought processes examined the phenomenon with the kind of logic that required words. Someone had come here, he thought. Two weeks or more, walking, they had come from either Eagle Grove or Bennington, through the Saddlebacks, here, to this place, to make a house.

It made no sense.

He started to turn away. He could go well around.

Then a sharp movement at the house caught his attention.

The door had opened. Somebody had come out onto the porch. Shed's vitals jerked, because it was a *child*—a skinny, pale, blond-haired boy wearing raggedy pants. He had a bucket in his hand, but his eyes—clearly an amazing green even at the distance—spotted Shed at the same time Shed saw him.

The bucket dropped. "*Momma!*"

Momma? That meant a woman. But of course there would be a woman. Shed's body drew up inside and something lurched sluggishly, and pulsed. He knew he ought to get away as quickly as possible. People were all a danger to him now. People in houses . . . towns . . . wanted him dead. He had been hunted so long that the impulse to run was practically the only reaction he now had to other white people. Run from them or kill them, that was what you did.

At the house, the door moved slightly. A second figure —another tyke, pale-eyed and fair, like the first!—peered from inside. Then, farther back in the doorway, was the woman.

Shed's chest felt like it collapsed as he saw her, because she was tall, slender, with long, loose-flowing hair of the same incredible color as the children's. She was young, he could see that, and the loose-fitting gray dress did not conceal the ripeness of her. Her lips parted and her eyes were wide, the same vivid hue of the children, with the fright of a wild, gentle creature in them.

Then he saw the gun barrel.

Her voice tattered. "Go away! Leave us alone!"

Just as well. Just as well. He turned and hopped the ditch.

"Wait!" the woman's voice cried despairingly.

He looked back over his shoulder.

Her shoulders slumped. "Help us! *Please!*"

Shed took a slow breath. It could be a trick. There could be the man hiding, waiting to kill. But he did not think so. He sensed that there was no man here. Just this woman, and the boys. And the sight of the woman up there made every cell of his body cry out.

He recrossed the ditch and trudged up the muddy slope to the house. The woman sent the boys inside. She remained on the porch, the gun in her hands. She was pale as death, and trembling. She held the gun as if she knew how to use it, Shed noticed, but it was a very old gun. The woman interested him much more. As he drew near, he saw that she was taller than he had imagined, almost his own height, with a slender strength about her and fine breasts. But she was not fat. She would be strong, but a man would be able to dig his hands in and hurt her and feel bone and muscle, not fat, and she would be wild and hard and enough . . . more than enough—

"Stop there," she ordered. He had reached the foot of the three steps to the porch. "Who are you?"

Shed licked his lips. At times like this he sometimes wondered if words would come—if he still had a voice and the memory of how to make the sounds. "Won't hurt you," he said.

"Just go away. Leave us alone."

"You said come help you!"

She stared at him, her face twisting in indecision. He decided it for her. He reached up and caught the gun and wrested it from her hands. She burst into tears. He turned and threw the old gun down the slope. It sailed over the garden plot, turning end over end, and hit in some shale and mud and then slid out of sight.

Pushing the woman out of the way, Shed went into the house.

There was no man. He saw that first. It was a single room, larger inside than the exterior suggested, with a stone fireplace to the right and an eating table, some chairs, and two beds, one in the far back corner and one in the front. There was a crib near the front bed. The floor was littered, suggesting turmoil, and he could see no sign of stored food. The only fuel for the fireplace was a small pile of soggy sticks. The two towheaded boys stood fearfully near the fireplace, as if they could hide behind the old rocker there.

Shed walked to the crib. There was a little girl in it, awake. She was almost too big for the crib and would have looked funny in it if she had not been so obviously sick. The sweet odor of fever issued from her blanket and her pink nightdress. Her long, yellow hair was pasted to her face with sweat. Her eyes appeared dazed. Shed touched her forehead. She was afire.

Behind him, the door closed. He turned. The woman stood there as if at bay, watching him.

"Where's your man?" Shed asked.

"He . . . died."

"When?"

"A week ago."

"Fever?"

"Yes."

He pointed down at the crib. "Girl-child has it too."

"I know. We're trying to help her."

Shed glanced at the boys, seeing their pallor. "You probably all had it. One gets it, everybody gets it. Fever's like that."

The woman said nothing and the boys stared.

"You bury him?" Shed asked.

She shuddered. "Yes."

"You got food?"

"Not now. We ran out. We don't have anything."

"How you expect to live without food?" Unaccountably, he was angry.

"I don't know," she said. "We've *tried.*"

"Shouldn't come out here. Don't know how to do things. You *want* to die?"

"Help me with my baby! Just help me with Elizabeth and then you can go! We'll find food somehow."

Shed unslung his packs. "Get some water. Get some water down her. That's first. She's bad sick, but try."

"She just throws up—"

"Put it down her anyhow!" He dropped the heavy packs onto the table. "Got some meat in there. Chaw on it some. Get your fire up, get water on. Boil."

The woman looked at him with great, frightened eyes. Then she looked at the packs. She hesitated.

Shed pointed. "In that 'un."

She struggled with the straps and then got the pack flap opened. She pulled out the wrapped strips of venison, dried well now and like varnished rope. With a quick, surprising motion, she ripped off two chunks.

"Boys," she said.

The two boys hurried forward and took the meat and attacked it as if they were starving. She watched them for a moment, then lifted a piece to her own mouth and ripped off a bite with strong white teeth. Her breasts rose and fell sharply with the excitement of the food. She was almost wild, Shed thought. She was a beautiful animal.

She looked up fearfully, as if sensing his desire. "You have—enough to share?"

"I'll get more food," Shed told her.

"Where? How?"

He felt a stab of disgust with her stupidity. He pointed toward the door. "Out there." He held out his big hands, palms up. "With these."

"Who are you?"

"Name of Shed."

"What do you want?"

The question startled him. "You ast me to help."

She hung her head. "I'm sorry."

Because she was so heartbreakingly beautiful, he kept his tone gentle. "What would your name be?"

"Slocumbe."

"First name."

"Faith."

Shed pointed to the crib. "Her?"

"Elizabeth."

"How old?"

"Two."

He glanced toward the two boys. "Them?"

"Jason is the oldest. And Richard."

"Jason, how many years have you got?"

The boy looked scared. "I'm nine."

"Richard?"

The smaller boy showed no response, but kept chewing at the meat.

Jason said, "He's seven."

Shed turned back to Faith Slocumbe. There was an unaccountable anger in him. "You hadn't ought to of come here," he told her.

"The land didn't belong to anybody."

"It's hard land. It's not fitten for tykes."

"We wanted to have a farm."

"*Here?* On this land?"

"The Homesteader Act—"

"You can't farm this land," Shed cut in angrily. "It's rocks and ice, too cold or too flooded, and then when it's hot it's so hot you can't breathe."

"We were going to have cattle," Faith Slocumbe said falteringly.

"Cattle? With panthers and wolves and grizzlies? You crazy?"

"Maybe it isn't the best land in the world, but it's the only land we could possibly have! Don't you understand that? Do you think we *wanted* to climb up here and be alone and have the snow close us in, and sit by the fire and look out and see those wolves howling at the window?" She shuddered. "Where else could we *go?* This land was *free.*"

"Free," Shed countered, "for them that can live in it."

"Men like you?" she flared.

"Awyep," he breathed. "Men like me."

"People like us deserve a chance too. Harold said we could make a go of it—"

"Harold?"

A shadow crossed her face. "My—husband."

"Uh," Shed grunted.

"He said we had to take a chance. He said this country has to be built. He said we could make a go of it. He said he wanted to *try*. Don't you see what he meant?"

"Awyep," Shed said. "Only, he's dead, ain't he."

He would stay, he decided, long enough to accomplish what he wanted. Then he would go on, because there was still that feeling of pursuit somewhere behind him.

Night was coming on as he walked out of the cabin a little later to get food. He was angry with the woman, but perplexed. He walked up the mountain in the dying light and got a clean, straight-on shot at a small buck. He dressed out on the spot, eating part of the liver and drinking some blood, and then carried the carcass down to the cabin. He carved off steaks and took them inside and then, angry and wanting to show the woman how much food a real man could supply, went out again and downslope to the stream. The light was going fast but there was still enough. Lying belly down on the wet bank, he could see the silver and amber flashes of the trout in the water. Quickly, stabbing down, he caught two of them with his hands, stunned them on a rock, and gutted them. On the way back up the hill he stopped at the ruined garden and found some seed potatoes that had been missed, dug them up, cut away the bad parts, and took them along. He found some wildflower greens and a pocketful of berries. The moon was just coming up above the sharp angle of the mountain as he went into the cabin again.

The fireplace fire crackled. The smell of roasting venison was thick in the air. The boys, watching the meat sizzle, looked brighter. Shed put the other things on the table, and, ignoring the woman for the moment, prepared the greens. Then he dug out his coffee that he had been saving for two months. Faith Slocumbe gave him a quick, nervous smile of thanks.

He went to the old rocker by the fireplace and sat down to rest himself. He felt achy; the place where he had fallen and broken something in his back two years ago was sorer than usual. The hurts didn't go away any more as they once had. The years in the mountains had taken a toll. He was forty-one. He felt older.

Being in a real house, however, beside a real fireplace in a genuine rocking chair, eased him. It had been a long time. He felt his spirits rise slightly and he wished he had not broken his old pipe. If he had the pipe now, and tobacco, he would have smoked.

The crib with the little girl in it was in his line of vision, and he wondered what he was going to do about the little girl. There was no telling how sick she really was, but he knew it was plenty bad. The fever might take her right out, as it had her father. The woman would crack open if the little girl went, too, Shed thought. Right now she was going mainly on nerve and the need to do whatever she could to keep the cubs alive. Take a cub . . .

It was not a pleasant thought. It motivated Shed to turn in the chair and look at Faith Slocumbe.

She was at the table, arranging things. Supper was almost ready. She was intent on her task, her arms bared for the work and a film of perspiration silvery on her upper lip. As she moved, her heavy breasts strained against the thin material of her dress, and as she moved again Shed saw the full outline of her long leg under the skirt. Things moved around inside him, as they had earlier. He was going to have her, he decided. He wondered if she would scream and try to make a mess of it. He hoped not. If he could avoid it, he did not want to make anything really bad happen to her.

He remembered the last time he had had a white woman. She had fought him, and he had been enjoying it for the first little while, but then he had had one of his spells. The next thing he had known, she was already dead and not at all pretty any more. He had regretted that.

Shed had his spells at irregular intervals. Some were very small and he possibly missed them altogether. Some were only a little bigger, and he might, for example, wake up in the middle of the day and be standing very still, or lying on the ground, and a minute or two—or an hour—had vanished. The big spells sometimes lasted several hours, and often included something like the woman and what had happened to her. Other times, when he was alone, he awoke with a feeling of strangulation, and sometimes he had bitten his tongue and gagged on his own blood.

As far as Shed knew, he had had the spells all his life.

Faith Slocumbe moved past his chair to swing the meat off the fire. He almost reached out for her. His hands itched to feel her flesh. He resisted.

With quick, sure movements, she removed the meat and put it on a platter. She carried it to the table. "All right, boys," she told the tykes, who were already standing there with greedy eyes. She lowered her tone. "All right, Mister Shed," she added.

They ate by candlelight, Shed and the boys wolfing it down, Faith Slocumbe eating slower and more carefully. They did not talk. When Shed looked at the woman, if she happened to be looking his way, she lowered her eyes quickly, startled. When the meal was finished, she wordlessly brought him his mug of coffee. She did not take any for herself. He knew there was enough for another cup or two, but did not urge her to share. If she wanted to let him have it all, it was all right with him.

She tried to get the little girl to eat, offering her food on a spoon, in the crib. The child had a coughing fit and could not hold anything down. The boys went to their bed and climbed up, starting some kind of game with wooden blocks.

Shed stood and stretched. "Good," he said.

"I can't make her eat," she said. "If she won't eat, she can't get better."

"Maybe tomorrow," Shed lied.

She frowned and nodded.

"Only thing in the world," Shed told her, "a man could want after a supper like that would be his pipe."

"Smoke if you like," she said very formally.

"No pipe. No fixin's."

She thought about that a moment, then said, "We have a pipe. And some tobacco."

He looked at her.

She turned and went to a cabinet. She returned with an old pipe, rather heavy, and a tin.

"Your man's?" Shed asked.

"Yes."

"You want to let me use 'em?"

"I think he would want you to. You're helping us."

Very surprised, he took the pipe and tin to the rocker. There were matches and some old, dry-shredded tobacco in the tin. He stuffed the pipe and lighted it. The strong smoke filled his head. The pleasure was intense. He thought, I'm smoking your tobacco in your pipe, dead man. I'm sitting in your rocker in front of your fire. And in a little while I'm going to pleasure myself with your woman, too.

The thought of so completely taking a dead man's things pierced him to the quick with a feeling of power.

He took the strong smoke into his lungs and leaned back in the chair. The two boys left their bed and sidled over near him. The older, Jason, had a curious glint in his eyes. Richard, the younger boy, stared with a lusterless expression. He showed absolutely nothing. His face had an uncanny smoothness, as if no thought or feeling had ever perplexed it.

Jason asked, "You like to smoke, Mister?"

"A powerful lot," Shed told him.

"That's my paw's stuff."

"Awyep."

"Are you a mountain man?"

"I been called one."

"Are you an outlaw?"

"Been called that, too."

Jason was impressed. "Which?"

"What?"

"Which are you really?"

"They don't shut each other out, boy."

"I guess the way you got us food and stuff, you know everything."

Shed was amused. "Enough." He chucked the younger boy under the chin. "Right, boy?"

Richard's head jiggled slightly, but he said nothing and did not change expression an iota.

Shed turned back to Jason. "Don't your bud talk?"

"Nope."

"He don't talk?"

"Nope."

"How come?"

"I dunno. He never has. He can. He just don't. Sometimes he makes these little grunts. And he hears you. If you yell, he jumps. But he don't talk. Never."

Shed leaned closer to Richard, beginning to understand the vacant expression. "So you don't talk, huh?"

Richard stared.

"Just listen an' watch," Shed mused.

"His brain got damaged when he was borned, a doctor said," Jason told him.

Shed studied the smaller boy. It touched him, the knowledge that another human being had some kind of a head problem too. He looked hard into Richard's eyes, and in the vacant pupils he saw his own face reflected. Him and me are alike, Shed thought.

Jason drew his attention back. "Do you hunt all the time, Mister?"

"To eat," Shed told him.

"You trap?"

"Awyep."

"My paw was gonna trap."

In the crib, the little girl began coughing. It started

with a gasp and a sharp, wet intake of air, and then became a rasping fit, each breath a drawn-out fight, with the sound of chalk held at the wrong angle to a slate. Faith Slocumbe rushed over. Shed got up and moved to her side. The little girl was choking. Already she looked blue around the lips. Shed pushed the woman aside, grabbed the little girl up, and tossed her onto his shoulder. He banged her hard on the back, and then again. She cried out and spat a little glob of mucus onto Shed's arm. Then she began to quiet down, breathing better.

Shed rocked her in his arms, standing there by the crib. The woman watched him. Gratitude chased the fright from her eyes.

"She's all right," Shed said.

"Yes."

It felt very strange to stand there with the tiny weight of the little girl in his arms, the blasting fever-heat radiating from her body into his chest, the woman and the two boys watching him with mute dependency. He did not know how to act. He did not know for certain that he liked it.

A little later, Faith Slocumbe told the boys to go to bed. They obeyed, and whispered to one another for a little while. Shed smoked another pipe and rocked. Faith Slocumbe hovered over the little girl, and then later came to sit on the edge of the raised hearth, her hands clasped over her knees as she stared tiredly into space.

The fire settled down and the boys went to sleep and the little girl was still in the crib. Shed's body whispered to him as he watched the woman. He could not wait for it much longer.

She said, "You've helped us so much."

He shrugged.

"No," she said. "It's true. I prayed and you came. I think God must have sent you."

"Don't talk like that," Shed told her.

She flinched from his tone. "Why?"

"God don't send people like me. You don't know about people. Don't talk about no God."

"But you've saved our lives."

"Saved nothing. It ain't over with yet."

The firelight was golden on her bare arms. "I know we can't stay here."

"You know that, do you."

"Yes. We have to go. I hate to leave . . . him. But we can't stay."

Shed said nothing. It was almost the time, and the rich timbre of her voice, lowered to avoid disturbing the children, only inflamed him.

She asked, "Can you help us leave here?"

He was startled. "Help you?"

"Get to Eagle Grove."

"You can't get to Eagle Grove, not with these tykes—that one sick."

"We can't stay here."

"It's two weeks or more, walking. Even for men."

"We walked in."

Ah, she was hard. Not hard like a man, but there was courage inside. She had walked in with her man and her cubs, and she would walk out, if he let her. She would walk out or die. She was that kind of woman.

But Shed pointed out, "You didn't walk this time of year. Not with snow in them passes."

"We could go on the river, then."

"Not this time of year."

Her lips set. She looked very beautiful, very determined. "Take us as far as Bung's Ferry. They have boats there. Other people come through. We can get someone to help us from there."

Shed shook his head.

"You must!"

"It's two days to Bung's. Three, with these tykes. You can't make it. And that ain't my direction anyway."

"You have to take us there. I'll do anything you want if you'll just take us that far."

Shed met her eyes. There was silence, and he heard her breathing, the whisper of charred flakes falling red hot in the fireplace embers. He listened, too, to his own pulse.

Faith Slocumbe's eyes changed as she saw what he was thinking.

Shed allowed the minute to endure, and refused to change his expression. Within himself there was an inferno building.

She stood. She had become terribly pale. "All right."

He kept his gaze full on her, needing no words.

Her large, graceful hands moved up to her throat. Her fingers reached the top button of her dress. She opened that button, and then the next one. Her eyes still refused to leave his, although her torment had begun to hammer its way into murky view.

"Won't do you good," Shed said thickly.

She was like a cool statue, and her fingers continued to open buttons. She was frighteningly calm.

"You got no bargain," Shed raged. "I'll have you anyhow. You can't give a man what he's already made up his mind to take."

The dress was now unbuttoned to the waist. Her lips parted in an awful expression he could not read, and very gently she moved to slip the material off her shoulders. It spilled down, and the startling white of her breasts was revealed. Shed drew in his breath sharply, a pain in his throat. She was far more lovely than he had imagined—more than any experience he had ever known.

She stood waiting for him, her arms at her sides in submission.

A small stick broke and showered sparks in the fireplace.

Shed rose unsteadily. He moved toward her and reached. With a gesture that was infinitely selfless—one that tried desperately to be something of tenderness and acceptance—she raised her arms to meet him.

There was a spell then, just a little one, but something tearing in his brain. And then he had dragged her to the bed—the dead man's bed—and had torn her clothing away, and his own, and had her beneath him. Her eyes were huge with fear and pain, but he was dimly aware that she moved—she opened her legs to him in a spasmodic movement—and he plunged down and then up and into her, tearing at her, on the black chasm of another spell, and he knew, as he savaged her, that she was trying as much as she could, helplessly, to help him destroy her if that was what he wanted to do.

When finally he had finished with her, and let her go, she cried without sound for a little while. Then she got up and went to the crib and checked on the little girl and tried to give her some water. She was very gentle and very quiet. She had not made a sound during any of it. The boys had not been awakened. Watching her, Shed realized that she had been concerned about this, had been thinking of the children all the time.

He could not understand her. He could not understand any of it. She was beyond his experience and beyond his comprehension, just as were the little girl who might be dying and the boy Jason with his funny questions and the other boy, Richard, with his brain damaged like Shed's own.

Shed was filled with wonderment.

TWO

In the night there was light rain that made a sifting sound on the roof, and in the morning it was over and the little girl was worse. She lay still in her crib, staring up at Shed as her mother changed the gown that had been stained by sputum from another coughing attack. Her fever was, if anything, higher. Shed had never felt a body that radiated such heat. Her skin was dry, like the surface of a stone that had been in the midday sun, and her eyes had a slightly yellowish cast. Her breath smelled strongly of a sweetly rotten decay. She took some water from a spoon and Shed allowed himself a particle of hope.

When she had finished, Faith Slocumbe drew a slow, deep breath and said, "I'll get food ready."

There was no hate in her tone. It was completely matter-of-fact, neither friendly nor antagonistic, and not even pained. Shed watched her begin preparing meat and stirring the small fire. He did not understand, and his anger simmered.

Despite the anger, he tried to speak in low tones, because the two boys still slept in the far bed. "How come you not to scream at me? Or cry?"

She brushed her long hair back with her hand, and did not face him. "I don't know. How am I supposed to act?"

The anger built. "I ain't your man. Your man is dead.

He's *just* dead. You're grieving. It wasn't any deal. You didn't give me nothing, because I took it, you didn't give it. That's what I do, I take. But there you stand, acting like it was—like it was—"

"Like it was all right?" And she turned.

"Like it was all right!"

Her eyes were the most amazing thing. Her eyes, and her total seeming calmness. Her cheeks were still pink, scoured sore by his beard. But she might not have been touched, from other appearances. And she looked at Shed with that incredible calmness.

"Or maybe," Shed raged, "it *was* all right. Maybe your man wasn't much of a man. Maybe you was wanting a real man. Maybe you act high and mighty and all that, but underneath you're like all the rest of them and it was all right, you liked it."

She would not speak.

"I know what I am," Shed told her. "I know what you think of me. I'm a God-damned mountain man. That's all I am. I eat what I can kill and I shit where I squat. There's people want me dead. I stink. I got bugs and now I've give them to you. Don't try to tell me it was all right. Don't try to fool me. I know what it was like for you. I know how decent women are. I did you, but it was no deal, I don't care *how* you tried to move and act like it was all right and you accepted me in you. I know you feel like you're full of puke, with my stuff in you. You don't fool me, because I *know*. You can act that way all you want, but any time I do you, I'm taking you; you're not giving me anything, because I don't want it, I know how I make you really feel, and it's no deal. *It's no deal.*"

She said nothing, and in the far bed the two boys sat

up, awakened by Shed's voice rising. Shed looked at them an instant, and then back to her, and her eyes defeated him. He turned and slammed out of the cabin.

The weather was not good. Low clouds scudded over the tips of the mountains, blocking out the sun. It was colder, and mud was everywhere. Shed walked angrily down the slope, got down behind some brush, and relieved himself. He shivered as the wind whipped his bare haunches.

He would get out, he told himself. They were not his problem. He could shoot another deer, dress it out for them, leave most of his salt, and get walking. Maybe they would survive and maybe they wouldn't. It didn't matter to him. Not at all.

Buttoning his clothes, he turned and started up the slope toward the house. He saw that one of the boys—the younger one, Richard—had come out to stand on the porch. He was urinating off the side of the porch, his little dilliwacker hardly showing through his pants.

Shed walked up to him. Richard turned and eyed him with his usual solemnity. —Brain damage, Shed thought. He's a little like me.

"That feel better?" Shed asked him.

The boy stared.

"Hell of a thing, having to get up and go out in the cold," Shed told him. "But a man can't hold it forever, right?"

The boy reached up and brushed at his own face, as if cobwebs were there. He kept his attention on Shed.

"Oh, you don't need to fret," Shed said. "I got it too, you know. I bet you didn't know that, did you. Awyep. Same kind of thing, boy. I don't know how you got yours and I don't know how I did, either. Do you ever forget things? I do. Don't worry. You'll get used to it. Man can get used to anything. I don't want you worrying about it, you hear?"

Shed paused and then reached out and pulled Richard down, sitting him on his knee. Richard grasped one of Shed's fingers in his hand, hanging on tight and watching him raptly.

"You can make it fine," Shed assured him. "Well, there'll be people call you names, act like you're shit. Pay no mind. You got a lot of things working your way and you remember it, right? You got you a momma. I never had a momma. You be good to your momma. You grow up strong, you hear? You're going to need to be strong.

"See, boy, people take what they can get. If you ain't strong, they take all your stuff. You eat good, get as big as you can. You'll be afraid—oh, sure, you'll be afraid plenty. But you'll be fine. Just don't let people walk on you. Just because you forget, or have spells, or can't talk or something, you just don't take nothing off of nobody. You fight if you have to. But you be your own man. You understand?"

Richard watched with the same solemnity, and put his thumb in his mouth.

Shed felt a surge of emotion that was unfamiliar. "I think you savvy what I'm saying to you. You might not talk good, but I bet you could talk if you wanted. You just don't want to bother, right? Hell. I can see that. Times I don't want to, either. You and me, we're a lot alike. That's why I sort of like you. Take ten years off of me and tack it onto you, we might be brothers. Then I could be your big bud, right? Then if some son of a bitch tried to make you feel like shit, I'd cut their guts out, right? You'd be all right then, boy!"

Richard reached out and rubbed soft fingertips over the harsh stubble of Shed's face.

"Feel it? Sure, you'll have a beard too one of these days. Sure you will! I recollect looking forward to mine coming in. And it came in. Lordy, lordy, I thought, 'Is my beard *ever* going to come in?' But it did. Yours will too. You're going to be just fine, boy. Don't ever let anybody tell you different."

The door of the house opened and Jason peered out. "My mother says it's time to eat breakfast."

Shed lifted Richard to his feet and set him on the porch. "Let's go eat, boy, all right? Eat? You savvy eat? Hell. You don't have to tell me. I *know* you savvy eat. Come on. Let's go get it."

At the table, Faith Slocumbe maintained her eerie calm. Shed wondered how long he could endure it. Then he realized he didn't have to endure it at all, because he was leaving. The idea cheered him: get the tykes off on a wild-goose chase, take her one more time and *this* time make her show what she really thought of him . . . and then get out.

His timetable for travel was not inflexible. It depended on the melting of snows, the opening of a certain pass to the north, how bad a stream was flooded, whether he found sign of other whites or of hostile Indians, whom he had to circle to avoid. But there was no time in it for trying to haul a woman and three tykes to someplace like Eagle Grove. That was out of the question. There was the matter of this thing pursuing him.

Take her physically once more, and then get out. That was the plan. He liked it.

"You boys want to be some help to me when you're through there?" he asked, feeling almost jovial.

"Sure!" Jason said eagerly. "What is it?"

Richard, naturally, showed no sign of anything, but continued to chase a piece of meat around his plate with his finger. He was a good boy, Richard, Shed thought. His kind of boy. They understood each other.

"Walk up the slope for me," Shed said. "Up there where the big rocks are, you'll find mushrooms. Pick a batch."

"Can you eat 'em?"

"They're the best you ever ate, boy."

Jason pushed back from the table. "We'll go right now, then. C'mon, Richard."

"You'll be careful up there," Faith Slocumbe said.

"Sure! Gimme a sack, huh?"

She went to a cupboard and got a gunnysack. Jason shrugged on his coat and helped his little brother with his. Richard looked up questioningly at Shed.

"Go on," Shed told him encouragingly.

"Yeah, Richard, c'mon!" Jason was already at the door.

Richard followed his brother out. The door closed. Jason, talking a blue streak, went off ahead, and his voice faded behind the house somewhere.

Faith Slocumbe said, "You're going to help us collect food for our trip?"

"Ain't no trip," Shed said, and stood to walk toward her.

Her expression tensed and her eyes darkened, but she stood her ground. God, the pride the woman had!

She said softly, unflinching, "If you won't guide us, we'll go on our own."

"No way."

"We can't stay here. We'll all die. Elizabeth has to have a doctor."

"I *told* you you can't make it out."

"Draw us a map."

"So you can die out there somewhere?"

"Die here or die there, what difference does it make? At least help us *try*."

"You'll stay here," Shed ordered.

"Then we go without you and without a map, too."

"I can't take you, woman—no matter how sick anybody is! People—want me. If I go into that town, they kill me."

"Would it be the same at the river?"

"Men there might kill me. If they didn't, the river would."

"You wouldn't have to take us down the river."

"*Someone* would!"

"Take us just that far. Please."

"I told you."

"Then give us a map."

"Woman—"

"Please!"

There was a small spell. He staggered. Involuntarily she reached toward him as if to help him. —*Help* him.

This made his rage break. He tore the front of her dress down. She took a step backward. He caught her and hurled her to the floor. She hit heavily, sprawling. He plunged down on her.

She did not fight.

In a while, the boys were coming back. Shed stood at the back window chink and watched them. This time, at least, Faith had broken a little bit. She had been crying a long time.

Shed turned to her. "I'll be going."

"I didn't fight you," she said.

"I told you: no deal!"

He went to the corner and quickly repacked his stores. He left most of the salt on the table, and the last powdery coffee. He felt vaguely that he wanted to make these gifts, but quickly rejected an impulse to speak of it.

He hoisted his packs onto his back. "You didn't fight because you know I'd kill you, and then where would the tykes be?"

She stood by the fireplace, her hands clasped as if in prayer. "Where will they be if you don't help us get out of here?"

He walked to the crib and looked at the little girl. Her breathing was funny: ragged and shallow. His hand touched her forehead. The same. She seemed asleep.

"I don't help people," he said angrily. "I stay on my own. I've lived this long by staying alone. People don't help out. They hurt, or kill. That's them, that's me. Don't expect anything."

She said nothing, but looked up to meet his gaze. And this time all the pain was very clear.

Stung, he walked to the door, slammed it back, and strode out.

She would not beg, he thought. She had done all she could and now she would stay here and bury the girl, and then the tykes, and then it would be her turn.

Well, it didn't matter to him.

He started down the hill. He could hear Jason yammering away to Richard up there behind the house somewhere. The temperature was moderating, a few blue holes had appeared in the clouds, and the thaw would go on. The way to the crossing at the Buttermilk would be possible; not easy, but just narrowly possible, if one were careful and strong.

But Bung's Ferry meant other men. It meant everything Shed had learned to skirt as widely as possible. They would try to cheat him or kill him or take any woman in reach. And even if they didn't succeed, the river would be waiting to try its hand at killing, too.

Long before, Shed had made river trips. He knew some of their ways. He had once turned back from an attempt in the Colorado. They said the Buttermilk made the Colorado seem tame.

He could imagine it: boiling brown water, icy, seething over hidden rocks, taking your boat so fast that everything was blurred, and hidden whirlpools and suck holes, rocks, unexpected falls, downrushing logs as big as a house—he shuddered. Even on the tamest river trips, he had been afraid. Water was one of the things that terrified him . . . one of the few.

He clambered down past the wrecked garden plot, taking a different route than he had used before. He stepped past some fallen rock and came upon an area where the rock had been cleared away and the ground smoothed. There was a crudely made wooden cross in the ground.

It surprised him, and he stood there for just a moment. It was her man, of course. Somehow, seeing the grave made her isolation more real.

Shed turned and looked back up toward the cabin.

The boys, not seeing him, were just trooping manfully in the front door. Jason was carrying the sack, heavy with mushrooms. Richard was carrying an armful of brilliant blue wildflowers.

Shed took a deep breath, and it hurt very deep.

The impulse was absolutely insane.

He fought it and then gave up.

His feet clomped loudly, angry, on the porch as he reached it, and the door flew open before he could reach for the latchstring. Faith stared out at him, her eyes wide with unreadable hopes.

"You can't take much," Shed told her bitterly. "A little food, clothes, that's all."

"I know," she said, as if she had known all the time.

Shed clomped into the house. "I'll carry Elizabeth on my back."

"Yes," she said, as if she had expected that, too.

"Well?" he shouted. "Hurry, then! We go now or we don't go at all!"

She flew to obey.

The high country in this time was vastly empty. In the summer, more whites would come, mostly impelled by the desire for quick gain through traps or gun-hunting for pelts. Small bands of Indians might still be encountered at any time, but they had mostly retreated to the west and south, driven by white encroachment or tricked with treaties that would last only until more gold was found, or more silver rumored, or the railroad changed its mind about where to expand next. Shed knew he might meet someone as he struck out southwest toward the Buttermilk, and he was alert and ready. But he thought the real crisis would probably come when he reached the river. There he *knew* there would be other men.

It went slower the first day than he had hoped. The two boys could not keep to his pace. At first he was angry with them, but then, seeing their pale fatigue and how hard they were trying, he relented and encouraged them, and shortened his own strides.

Faith Slocumbe kept up. Again Shed was amazed by her inner strength.

That night, they camped under rock ledges beside a cliff. Seep water dripped off slippery outcroppings, making the crushed shale slope treacherous. They were all wet, cold, and miserable. Shed risked a large fire, and felt a quiet inner gladness as he watched the faces—the boys intent and solemn, she with that curious calm—in the firelight.

He went out and snared a rabbit and robbed a hawk's nest of its new eggs, and brewed the last grains of coffee. On impulse, he offered Faith the cup from which he had been sipping the coffee. She looked at him with her questioning surprise clear in her expression.

"Take it," he said. "It's hot."

"I don't want to take your coffee," she said.

"I'm offering it."

"Thank you, but it's yours, and I know you need it, too—"

"Damn you, then," he said, and hurled the tin cup down the ravine so that *neither* of them had it.

Elizabeth was, if anything, a little better. Shed had stoically expected her to die on his back. Stretched out on a blanket pallet, however, she seemed more alert and watched the fire with interest. Faith offered her some of the boiled egg and she took it weakly, keeping it down. She also drank a few spoons of water.

Her cracked lips moved after the water, and Shed leaned low over her to hear what she said.

"Thank you."

"Don't thank *me,*" Shed told her. "It's just water."

She looked up at him with her mother's eyes. Shed felt her forehead, although Faith had just done the same thing. The flesh felt as hot as before. Shed thought: Go away, fever. You've had her long enough. Go on.

She might beat the fever, he thought now, because she was tough, like her mother. There was a chance. *Maybe* she could beat it.

Not that he really cared, he added to himself. A man who cared for anybody or anything, very much, was crazy. And he might have something wrong with his brain, but he was not that crazy. He knew better.

There was little talk. Exhaustion claimed the family soon after the food, and Shed sat over them until very late and the fire had burned down and the wolves talked in the great distance.

In the morning he got them started early. He pushed them harder. They were delayed a little while by a stream in full flood, having to walk far upstream to find a place to get across, a rocky area where the stream spread, tumbling with foamy white over a rocky bed. He was able to walk across the stream here, the water up to his waist, pulling him heavily and threatening to take him away. He carried each of them across.

When he put Faith down on the far side with the others, she immediately began walking around, picking up sticks.

"What are you doing?" he demanded.

"We'll need a fire for you to get dry."

"Damn that! We got to move."

She looked at the sky with its lead clouds blocking off the sun. The wind was light but cold. "You need to dry yourself."

For answer, Shed picked up Elizabeth, put her back into his shoulder sling, and strode off. The boys trooped wearily after him. Faith brought up the rear.

It was a little victory, but it pleased him. He knew that was a little childish, but it didn't matter. She might be strong and unique, but there were things only men could do or understand. Women were inferior, like animals, on the earth for the men. He had never been bossed by a woman and he never would be. Listen to a woman and she would boss you if she could. It was the first step toward cutting off your balls.

Later, in the afternoon, after it had gotten colder and his pants were frozen, he avoided thinking about her suggestion of a fire to dry himself.

There was a long slide area they came to a little later in the day, and it was a hard climb even for Shed. Partway up the slope, he had a medium-sized spell.

He was climbing, bent well over, using hands as well as feet for maximum traction, sweating hard and breathing hard and wishing he were at the top.

Then he was upside down, his face in the rocky dirt—pointed *down* the slope, with his feet higher, and he was on his belly, and there was dirt and blood in his mouth. He became aware of sounds. Elizabeth, tied on his back, was coughing and crying. Somebody else was crying, too. Somebody's hands patted at his head. The pats were random, light.

Dizzy, Shed managed to sit up on the steep slope.

Sharp little rocks bit his butt. Yellow stars swung through his vision and then everything came back. His heart was pounding fast.

He had fallen about a hundred yards, perhaps tumbling, down the slope. Why he hadn't gone all the way to the bottom was beyond him. He had hurt his mouth and possibly his bad leg, but not seriously. Coming down the slope toward him, running at a dangerous pace, were Faith and Jason.

Richard, the dumb one, had already reached him somehow. Dirty and disheveled, the tyke was the one who had been patting at him. As Shed sat up, however, Richard stepped back from him and stared in the usual vacant way. There were tears making brown gullies on his cheeks.

"I'm okay, boy," Shed told him, and discovered he had bitten his tongue badly, as usual. He reached out and patted Richard. "I'm fine, boy."

He unslung Elizabeth and checked her over. She had gotten dirt in her face and hair, but the coughing was subsiding and she was more frightened than hurt. He was just finishing the examination when Faith and the older boy reached his side.

"What *happened!*" she asked breathlessly.

"I slipped," Shed lied.

"You turned, and it looked like you took a step back. Richard was right behind you. When you fell, you took him with you. Both of you—and you with Elizabeth on your back—slid and bounced, and slid and bounced—" She put her hands over her face and began to shake.

Shed looked at Richard, who showed nothing. He had stopped crying. He had, Shed realized, fallen down the slope right with him, had gotten up while Shed was still unconscious, had *immediately* started trying to make him wake up.

Richard had been more worried about Shed than about himself.

Or at least that was how Shed saw it.

Shed left Elizabeth lying in her harness and picked Richard up. He swung him overhead so he could look him in the eye. "Listen, boy," he said sternly. "Don't you worry about other folks, you hear? You worry about *you!* You got that? Remember it! I'll take care of me, bud. You take care of you, right?"

Richard did not respond, so Shed put him down on his feet, turned, and got Elizabeth in the sling again. While he did this, he was busy swallowing the blood coming from his bitten-through tongue. He did not want the damned woman to see that. Nobody understood his spells. Even men didn't. A woman would make a mess, just knowing.

Shouldering Elizabeth, he turned to the slope again. "Go," he said, which was as much as he could trust himself to say without spitting blood.

Her forehead wrinkled, Faith obeyed and they began climbing again. Shed wondered how much she knew.

The late of the day took a savage toll, and when they rested it was long after dark. The boys collapsed against soggy tree trunks in the gully Shed had selected for the night camp. Shed unharnessed Elizabeth, mechanically checked her fever, could not see any change, and sank to his haunches to catch his breath. Faith, a shadowy figure that wobbled with every step, gave the little girl water from her hands, then knelt in the earth to begin collecting chips of wood for the fire.

"No," Shed said.

She looked up.

"No fire," he told her.

"Why?"

"People."

"Where?"

He pointed. "Listen."

Beyond the tinkle of the creek nearby, off in the distance, was a dull roar. It had grown so slowly and steadily that it would not be noticed unless one listened for it. It pervaded, steady and huge and mysterious, like the slumbering breath of a giant.

"The Buttermilk," Shed told her.

"We could go on," she said. "Get there."

"No."

She seemed too weary to ask why this time. She sank back to a sitting position.

In the dark, the children already slept.

Watching the woman, Shed felt an insane pulse of desire. It was like that sometimes. Out of the very tiredness came a tension, and you only relieved it with your fist, or with a woman. But something made him not want to do anything to her tonight. She had done everything he asked of her and she was exhausted. It was not fair to ask more.

He got dried meat out of his pack, and offered some to her. She took it and ate. He thought about tomorrow. There would be men to face tomorrow. A black mood stole through him with this prospect. He would handle them, he thought, however they had to be handled. But he did not have to like it.

The moon appeared through black vees of rock, low, its light a strange orange on broken bluish clouds. The light scattered and paled, mixing with the rumble of the Buttermilk, as if a dragon slept beyond the rocks somewhere and its breath was a fire that tainted the sky.

THREE

At the first sight of the river, something shriveled inside Shed, and he had to fight a great impulse to turn his back to it and run.

He had left Faith and the children at the gully campsite, coming on alone to survey the situation. Moving at his own pace, he had needed only a few minutes to come through the vee of rocks, across a shallow cliff, and through the tumbled slag and erosion wreckage, climbing, to this position which gave him a view of the Buttermilk, and Bung's Ferry.

In the first moments, he could look only at the river. He looked, and stark fear rose up inside him and screamed to get out.

It had never been this high. Although Bung's Ferry had been built in a gentle canyon where the river was wide and should never move very fast, the Buttermilk curled through the canyon like a hideous brown snake, a hundred yards wide, boiling, carrying billows of froth, tree branches and chunks of debris. There were no hidden rocks close beneath the surface here, and yet the river *still* hurled up spray, broke in blood-colored chop and whirlpools. Shed tried to follow one tree trunk sweeping downstream, but it went from his far left, when he first spied it, around the bend a half mile to the right, in an incredibly short time.

The Buttermilk had gone crazy.

Bung's Ferry ordinarily consisted of two log buildings, with attached docks, high on either steep bank of the placid water. But the river had risen to hide both docks, if there were docks left at all, and the building on the far side was simply gone, carried away. The river boiled around the building on this side, and had already torn one wall off of it. The rest trembled, appearing ready to go at any moment.

The cable, used to guide the big raft across the river, was strung higher. Ordinarily, a man could not throw a rock high enough from the ground to hit it, and it was strung from cliff to cliff, bolted into bedrock, and ropes hung down like trolleys to guide the raft. Today the cable sagged in the middle to within ten feet of the boiling water surface.

The din was continuous and deafening.

Watching it, Shed shrank inside. He didn't like water at any time. This was no longer even a river. It was an insane thing, tearing over trees, buildings, rocks, *mountains* for all he could know, taking out everything.

As he lay on his belly, hidden in the rocks overlooking the scene, he first tried to think of alternatives. Instinctively he rejected leaving the woman and children where they were. It was just as impossible to go back to the cabin. They simply could not make it overland to Eagle Grove. The town of Bennington was even farther.

Trying to delay a decision, Shed studied the terrain surrounding Bung's Ferry, looking for the men.

He did not see them, but he spotted a thrown-up shack below his position, on ground slightly higher than the ferry site. Smoke whispered from a tin chimney pipe. The big raft had been manhandled out of the water and up onto the sandy dirt nearby, and two large wooden boats, each about fifteen feet long, with wide bottoms, lay turned over in the pale sun. So the men were here, all right, holed up, waiting.

Shed thought about it, then turned and went back down the way he had come.

The two boys were still asleep, tumbled on the ground just as they had dropped late the night before. Faith was bent over Elizabeth. She looked up, her fear and worry clear in her expression, as Shed neared her.

"She's worse," she said.

Shed squatted to verify it for himself. The little girl's eyes were closed. Her skin had a yellow cast. A touch of pink sputum clung to the corner of her mouth. Shed touched her forehead with his hand and jerked it away with involuntary shock. She was afire.

"We have to get her to a doctor or she'll die!" Faith said.

"We've know'd that," Shed snapped. "She might die anyhow."

"But she's worse! We have to hurry! —Did you find someone to take us? Is there a boat? Is the river—"

"The river's bad. Worse'n I ever saw."

She looked at him.

He said, "River'll kill us."

He was talking nonsense now, and he knew it: he was talking like the boy he had killed for his gun last fall. But with a river it was *true*. A river was not like a mountain.

It moved. It tricked you. It sucked you under. You could not predict it.

Faith said, "We have to go on."

"I said no. I meant no."

"Then we die here."

"No."

Faith looked down at Elizabeth and her voice cracked. "She'll die. Soon. And then the boys will get it, Jason and Richard—"

"No! Richard ain't getting it."

"And then me—"

He grabbed her arm, twisting it hard. "No! *He* ain't getting it and *you* ain't getting it! He's tough. Richard's tough. He's like me. Never sick. And you ain't getting it neither. Nobody is. Nobody's getting any God-damned fever while I'm around to hold it off. Now you shut up!"

She sank back, staring into space. She looked, for the first time, beaten. And it shocked him.

—shocked him into seeing she was right.

He thought about it. Ah, God. He was afraid.

He got to his feet. "Wait. I'll be back for you in a little while."

There were two men.

Shed waited patiently, in hiding, and verified this.

They looked like they might have been stamped out with a cookie cutter. Both wore dark-blue pants and shirts, faded brown jackets, floppy hats, heavy boots, revolvers strapped on their hips. One had a heavy black beard and the other's beard was grayer but of the same shape. They walked out of the shack together, one picking his teeth and the other loading a pipe. One was slightly taller.

The taller one had a pet cat, black and mangy-looking, that followed him around. Whenever he stopped, as he did at water's edge, hands on hips, staring across toward the other side, the cat walked around and around his feet, rubbing against his legs.

The sight filled Shed with disgust. He had always hated cats. They always got to this kind of false, fawning adoration. All the rubbing and pressing made him feel sick at his stomach.

The two men seemed to have nothing to do. They walked around aimlessly, stretching, and then stood by the overturned boats, talking without gesture or evident emotion.

Satisfied that there was no one else around, Shed left his watching place and climbed down the hill, approaching the ferry through a rocky cleft in the hillside. He had left his Navy .36 revolver in camp, and carried his rifle loosely in his right hand. His skinning knife was in his belt. Going down to the level of the river, he tripped on a tree root and fell heavily, almost losing the knife, and tearing a hole in the left leg of his trousers. He was muddy, winded, and raggedy when he took care to walk slowly out of the fallen rocks into the open to approach the two men.

The shorter man saw him first and said something to his partner. The partner, holding and stroking his damned cat, turned and watched Shed with interest. Shed's bad leg was aching from the fall, and he allowed the limp to exaggerate itself.

"Mornin'!" the shorter man called.

"Mornin' to you, sir," Shed panted, walking up to their spot beside the boats.

"Look like you tangled with something."

"Aw, tripped back there. Near broke my neck."

The taller man, stroking his cat, asked, "You fall a lot, do you?"

"More'n I wish," Shed said, forcing the stupid grin.

The taller man grinned back. "Who might you be?"

"Name of Shed. John Riley Shed. You?"

Neither of them showed recognition of the name. "Mashrow and Glass," the taller one said. "I'm Mashrow, this's Glass."

"You run the ferry?" Shed asked.

"We do when we can. You don't see anybody else around, do you?"

"Well, I know it's named Bung's Ferry. I thought maybe there'd be a Mister Bung."

Mashrow tossed his pet cat to the ground and chuckled. "That was a long time ago, old timer."

They were not that much younger than Shed, and the tone of voice was insulting. Shed held his temper. "So you two fellers are it?"

"That's a fack."

"How does a man git a ride?"

Glass spat. "He don't."

"Oh?"

"You blind? Look at that river!"

"Well, I thought maybe the raft—"

"With this current, that cable'd snap in a minute if you tried to send the raft across tied to it."

"Well, I wasn't thinking to go across. I need to go down the river."

Glass's lip curled. "It narrows. Raft would stick—even if a man was dumb enough to try it."

"How about one of these here boats, then?"

Glass and Mashrow looked at each other. They had relaxed now, clearly figuring they had a loony mountain man on their hands. A look passed between them that said they would have some fun.

"Where," Mashrow asked, "do you aim to go?"

"Eagle Grove."

"In a hurry, I suppose?"

"Yes sir, I am."

"How much do you figure you might pay to use one of these here boats?"

Shed began to tire of it. "How much do you ask?"

"Since the boat ain't likely to make it any more'n the man that takes it, I'd say a hundred dollars would be about right, wouldn't you, Mister Glass?" Mashrow was having a fine time.

Glass chuckled. "I'd say that was about right, Mister Mashrow."

Mashrow nudged one of the overturned boats with his toe. At close range they looked like quite enormous boats, probably sixteen feet long, very wide and high, made of stout oak timbers and planks. Lying on the ground nearby were sets of oars and push sticks.

Mashrow said, "If you got a hundred dollars, we might talk business."

There was just no use in prolonging it.

Shed raised his rifle, which was already cocked, and shot Mashrow point-blank in the chest. He saw the man's stunned expression through the gush of black smoke from the muzzle. The smoke also gave him an instant's added confusion to get out the skinning knife. He stepped forward and drove the blade into Glass's midsection, going in to the hilt. Glass screamed and fell off the knife, flopping on the ground.

A small spell made the earth tilt and something flash painfully in Shed's skull, but almost instantly it was better again. Getting to his feet, he grabbed Mashrow's collar and dragged him to the boiling edge of the water. He threw Mashrow in. He then dragged Glass down and threw him in after the other man. The current took the body, as it had the other, and sucked it immediately under.

Shed kicked dirt over the mess by the boats, reloaded his rifle, cleaned the skinning knife, and headed back for the family.

"No one there, after all," he said cheerfully in reply to Faith's questioning gaze.

"At the ferry?" she asked.

"Awyep. Nobody around. They must of gone off when the river come up."

Faith looked at him thoughtfully, but said nothing. He helped gather up provisions. He wondered if she believed him.

A few gray clouds had begun to gather overhead when he led them back to Bung's Ferry. The two boys, knowing the way by the sound of the Buttermilk's roar ahead, led the way. They scrambled along excitedly, not showing the fatigue that had made them droop only a little while before. It made Shed feel a little better to see them. The killing had left him with a dry, empty feeling in his gut.

He was carrying Elizabeth, and Faith was last in line

through the broken rocks that blocked view of the river itself. As he stepped out onto the rocky downslope that led to the water's edge, he saw that the boys had stopped abruptly, as if transfixed by the Buttermilk's ferocity. Over the engulfing roar of water, he heard Faith's gasp as she came out of the rocks behind him. He turned.

She had stopped, and her eyes were like lead. She was staring at the river.

"My God," she said.

Shed moved them into the cabin, and if Faith read the evidence and knew it had recently been occupied, she said nothing about it. Shed stoked more wood into the stove right away, to hide the fact it had already been working, and carried the coffee pot outside as if to wash it, burning his hand because it was already half full of fresh coffee that he could not admit. When he went back to the cabin, the boys had discovered the damned cat, and were playing with it.

"Have some coffee," Shed said, going to the cupboard. "Boys here left in a big hurry. We benefit."

Faith knelt beside Elizabeth's still form on the rope bed in the corner. She was trying to make the child take some water. "She's so weak now. So sick!"

"We'll eat," Shed replied. "I'll get some stuff and make medicine. We got time."

"Are we . . . going on the river then?"

Seeing her fear, he hesitated. He did not want to go on this river. The fear inside him was like a chewing snake. But they could not remain here indefinitely, even though the cabin was well provisioned. The two men he had killed might have friends somewhere nearby. And this other thing—this feeling that something or someone else was trying to close in on him—remained strong. He had to choose: go on, with the Buttermilk, or go back the way they had come.

He went to the door of the cabin and looked out at the river. He spotted something and gestured for Faith to join him at the door. She obeyed.

He pointed toward the sandy bank not far from the spot where the two big wooden boats were beached. A snag of some kind—a single heavy, twisted twig—stuck out of the wet sand at the very edge of the water.

"See that stick?" he said. "Buttermilk might be rising, might be going down. We'll watch that stick. It'll tell us."

"How long?" she asked. She didn't have to say any more. It was clear that the same kind of fear was in her. No one in his right mind would dare this plunging cataract, but the decision to turn back was just as hard. She was begging for a reprieve from the necessity of decision.

"We'll give 'er a few hours," Shed decided.

They ate, but with no enthusiasm. Shed left the cabin and climbed into the rocks and brush beyond the rocks. Alone, with his rifle, away from the crushing sound of the river, he felt a little better. He did his searching slowly.

Despite his concentration and the dread that the distant rumble of the river kept inside him, he was puzzled and preoccupied by the continuing sense that something else was also wrong. He could not figure this out. It was the same feeling that had made him leave his cave early.

He longed for his cave now. If it had not been for this strange feeling, he would still be there. He would have waited another two weeks. He might be hunkered there by the fire at this moment, gnawing some meat, killing a few of his bugs, pleasantly half asleep, waiting, instead of out here by this damned insane river, wondering whether he could dare it with his life.

But he hadn't waited. And he could not delay the decision about the river past tomorrow morning, either. He had learned long ago to trust and obey feelings such as this one. It said: *Something is coming*. He had to pay heed.

FOUR

When Shed returned to the cabin, it was afternoon. He took the things he had gathered into the cabin and prepared them. Faith hovered nearby, watching, as he laboriously split the green stem of the one plant and peeled out its marrow into the small cooking pan where other ingredients gathered.

"What will this do?" she asked him.

"Make her better," he grunted. "Maybe."

"What is it?"

"Medicine." He was astonished by her ignorance.

"I mean, what are these things you put in it?"

He touched some of the bright-colored vegetable fragments with the tip of the hunting knife. "Pine. Hickory pulp. Juniper. Mint."

She pointed to some small berries. "These?"

"I don't know a name for 'em."

"How can you be sure they're the right thing?"

"You don't need *names,*" he told her.

"I'm sorry. I was just worried—"

"What do names matter?" He was stung. "If I give you a name for this stuff, does it make it work better?"

"No, but you're going to give it to my child, and—"

"I don't have to! If you think I'm too ignorant, you just

say so. I can throw it away. It wouldn't be the first time somebody thought I was too ignorant."

"No! I want you to try to help her. She's so sick now—I want you to try to help her. Please."

"All right, then," Shed muttered, mollified.

He worked in silence for a few minutes. She watched.

Then—"Where did you learn this?" she asked.

"I don't know," he lied.

"From a friend?"

He got up abruptly. "We'll cook it now. You got to cook it down to a paste." He took the pan over to the red-hot stove and placed it on top. He walked out of the cabin.

The sight of the river shocked him anew. He was so angry with the woman that he had almost forgotten the river. Its raw, wet smell engulfed him as he walked across the wet sand toward the snag that was his level indicator. The sound was enormous, thudding into his bones and making them vibrate. He wondered how the rock walls of the canyon stood against this force. Pausing for an instant, he watched a tree, bigger around than a man, plunge down the center of the stream and vanish around the rocky corner that blocked view downstream a few hundred yards away.

The boys were playing on one of the boats. He walked over to them.

"Are we going?" Jason asked brightly.

"Maybe," Shed said.

"Is Momma inside?"

"Awyep."

"Are you mad at her again?"

Shed considered lying, but Jason's inquisitive eyes and Richard's dull stare unnerved him. "Your mother don't know much," he said.

"She cries a lot," Jason said.

"I'm fixing stuff for your sis," he replied bitterly. "So your momma says, did I learn it from a friend. Like when you're crazy you ever had a friend. Don't she know nothing?"

"I had a friend," Jason said. "His name was Alfred."

"I'll tell you about friends, boy. You can get roped in by friends. They trap you. They come around and trick you, go behind your back, lollygag around—" He saw the damned cat in the bottom of the boat with the boys. "—like *that* thing. Do you think that thing cares about you? Don't you know it'd eat your guts if it got a chance? I'll tell you something. A man don't need friends and he don't need any damned cat or anything else. He don't need nothing. You want to be free in your life? Either of you? Then you'd better trust your own self. Nobody else. Never. A man don't need nothing else but himself. You remember that."

Jason studied him wonderingly. "You never had a friend? Ever?"

"I don't need one. I don't want one!"

Jason stared. "Gosh!"

Shed reached out to Richard and roughly clucked him under the chin. Richard's head bobbled violently and tears sprang to his eyes.

"You," Shed said, "remember it too. You need to know it worse than your bud does, even. You're like me."

He went down to the water's edge. The frothy brown

moisture licked at the place where the twig stuck in the sand. The Buttermilk had risen a few inches.

It might be temporary, he thought.

A little later, he went to the cabin and the medicine was a thick paste. He let it cool and then held the little girl while Faith spooned the stuff in. Neither of them spoke.

Night came. They ate supper. The boys finally gave out, collapsing in sleep on blankets in the corner. Faith hovered over Elizabeth, who slept. She was still afire with the fever. Shed went outside and walked around, and then climbed the rocks and looked all around for any sign of a campfire. The earth was black, with traces of wet snow in the air. He thought about the river and ways of escaping it, and about his family. But then there was a spell, because he suddenly was on his face in the wet gravel and rock chips of the promontory, he tasted blood and he was thoroughly chilled all the way through, and aching, and when he sat up quickly, frightened, he was lightly coated with the snow that had sifted down upon him while he was away.

Stiffly, angry, he trudged back down to the cabin. Inside, the stove gave off a faint pink glow that showed the boys sleeping in their blankets, Faith and Elizabeth on the rope bed beneath piled quilts.

Faith watched him as he went to the stove and tried to warm numbed hands. He was very angry and sick of having spells. He would warm his hands and then he would take her, he thought, and hurt her as much as he possibly could, to make her pay. But, as often happened after a bad spell, he was engulfed by the need to sleep.

He stretched out on the floor, not bothering with his boots or a blanket or anything else, and accepted it.

In the morning, the twig shuddered under the pressure of six inches of water. Shed looked out at the Buttermilk, hating it. *Damn you,* he thought, *why didn't you go down in the night?*

The sky was murky and it was cold. The air tasted of possible snow. There was more debris in the river today and it was going faster, if anything.

Shed climbed to the high rocks again, wrestled with the decision, and climbed back down, returning to the cabin. He had been first up, but fresh smoke from the chimney told him the others were awake now.

The boys were playing with the cat again, Richard mostly watching while Jason did everything. Jason looked glad to see Shed. Faith was cooking something in a pan on the bright pink stove. She gave Shed a frightened smile.

"She's better."

Shed looked at the bed. Elizabeth lay quiet, but her eyes were open. He went over and felt her forehead. It was still very hot, but not quite as bad.

"She took a little soup," Faith said.

Hearing the hope in the woman's voice, Shed did not tell her that the medicine was good at driving down fever but was only temporary. By tomorrow or the next day, unless a better treatment could be found, the fever would be back again. The Indians used this remedy sometimes to make a man better for the time it took to prepare him for the death rites, or for kin to arrive from over the next hill. It was not permanent. Only a real doctor could hope for a permanent cure. The only real doctor was down the Buttermilk.

They ate some beans and meat.

"What do we do now?" Faith finally asked him.

"I don't know," he said.

"The river. Is it—?"

"Up."

Her face twisted.

"You come out and look," Shed said. "We got to decide."

"You can decide."

"No. You were the one that had to come. I don't decide alone now."

"But if we just can't do it—!"

"Come out and look."

She accompanied him to the bank. The roar of the Buttermilk buffeted them. Shed saw that her fear was as great as his own.

"I don't see how we can do it," she said finally.

He nodded.

"Do you?" she asked.

"I can go on by myself. Back the way we came a little, then around."

"Can you take us that way? We can walk—"

"No. You can't make it."

"We made it this far."

"Woman, walking here was like laying in your bed, compared to what would be ahead!"

"But we could—"

"No."

She bent, almost as if she was going to spring at him in attack. "But then what choice do we *have?*"

"You can stay here. There's food. Somebody'll come along."

"You'll stay with us?"

"No."

Her face twisted. "How *can* we stay here, with Elizabeth still sick and the river still rising? I don't even know where we are, exactly. —But, my God, I don't want to try a boat in this—this terrible current!"

Watching her, Shed hoped she would say they could not go on. But he was not going to say it for her. He was not going to make this decision.

Dull anger worked in him. They had to try the river, he saw, despite the odds, or Elizabeth was surely going to die very soon. He did not much want to watch Elizabeth die. He did not at all want to watch any of the others die. If the woman said they should go, and then they died, it was different; it was her own decision. He would not help her make this decision.

She straightened. "Which boat do we take?"

Shed got to his feet and grabbed the prow of the nearest wooden craft. It was very heavy, and sunken a bit in the wet ground. He heaved at it. It rocked and then slid a foot or so. The two boys scampered over and manfully grabbed the sides, trying to help. Faith got up and came over and pulled beside Shed. The boat seemed to break loose from a little suction created by its broad, veed bottom in the wet dirt, and started sliding easier. Staggering backward, Shed hauled it toward the river until the bank steepened and he knew another movement would plunge it in.

Signaling them to stand back, he got oars and push sticks and tossed them inside. The boat teetered on the brink of a foot-high drop, ready to commit itself to the water. Shed walked across the muddy clearing to the shack, went inside, and found the cat on the table pecking at leftovers from breakfast. He found the salt and coffee, and what he had really been looking for, a big roll of stout rope. He carried these back outside and stowed them under the front of the boat with his packs, tying them down.

Shouting over the roar, he explained how he wanted Faith in the front, with a paddle, and the children in the middle section. They would sit below the seats, on the floor of the boat, the boys on either side with Elizabeth wedged between them.

"If you have to pee or anything," he added, "you better do it now."

The boys stood at the edge of the river and solemnly tinkled.

Shed cut a length of the new rope and attached it solidly to the iron ring in the front of the boat. The other end he extended to a log half buried in the sand, lashing it firmly. Then he gently eased the boat off its teetering position.

It went into the water back first, with a brown splash. The current whipped the back end in against the slight embankment so that the entire side clung. Shed climbed down into the boat. It trembled under his weight, sloshing from side to side, and panic gusted through his belly. Hiding the fear, he angrily ordered the boys in, Jason first, then Richard. He got them hunkered on the bottom. Faith handed Elizabeth's bundled form over to him and he got her bedded down between the two boys. Jason was wide-eyed with apprehension, but Richard was as calm as ever. Shed grinned and touseled his hair for him.

Leaning on the bank, his feet in the boat, he explained to Faith how he would help her in and get her settled, then hand her his skinning knife. When he was in the back, and ready, she would cut the rope that kept them from being carried away from the bank. She was very pale, but she nodded to show she understood and was not backing out.

He reached for her hand to help her in.

She paused and stared at the front of the boat. Her hand, instead of going to him, flew to her mouth.

Puzzled, Shed looked to see what it was on the side of the boat, near the front, that she saw.

They had painted a name on the boat, bright black paint on weathered gray planks. It said DEATH.

Shed recoiled and looked up the slope toward the other boat. It had a name, too: MOTHER.

"Don't matter," he said. "I ain't hauling that other one clear down here, starting all over. Don't mean anything. God-damned fools that'd name a boat *Death!*"

"It must have been a . . . joke," Faith said slowly.

"God-damned fool joke, if you ask me! What kind of a joke is that? That's not a funny joke!"

Jason, from his position in the bottom, called, "What is it? What happened?"

"Nothing," Shed snapped. "Shut up."

He did not like it. He was not a superstitious man, but he knew facts. He knew that when the wild dogs cried at night, it meant the spirits were walking. He knew that the spirits of some men lived again in bears, and that was why some bears walked erect, remembering when they had been men. He understood how you could sometimes remember not only what had been, but what was yet to come.

A boat named Death. He did not like it at all.

"You said the men who run the ferry are nowhere around," Faith said. "If the river got them, somehow, the joke was . . . on them."

The words hit Shed with a little thrill. Mashrow and Glass had painted the names, he thought. Mashrow, probably because he was the type. They had probably painted the names, laughing how all passengers would beg *please* to use the boat named Mother, and not the one named Death. And then Mashrow and Glass would put people in the boat named Death and tell them weird stories and scare them out of a year's growth, and, afterward, laugh about it when they were drunk.

Maybe that was it. Maybe not. Whatever the true reason, Mashrow's joke had come true for *him,* not for others.

It was Mashrow who was dead. And Glass. The boat had lived up to its name for them, all right. So now there was no more . . . evil . . . no bad luck left, and the name had—the name had been all used up.

The name of the boat could be anything he wanted it to be.

He heaved a breath of relief.

Faith was watching him.

"Come on," he told her. "Get in." He gave her his hand.

Awkwardly, the boat tipping sluggishly, she got to the front. She was frightened but trying not to show it. She had a long, awkward paddle in one hand and the skinning knife in the other. She watched Shed for instructions.

Shed clambered back to the rear, the boat tipping this way and that with every movement. The God-damn thing was too tippy, he thought. It wanted to get him. It was aptly named. But then he lost his temper and hurled that kind of thinking out of his mind.

Getting his fists around the rough handle of the oar, he wedged his feet into the side timbers. He felt solid and ready on the back bench. He looked at the ferry site, seeing that no sign remained of what had happened. He looked at the boys and the bundled form between them and at Faith, who crouched ready with the knife. The boat vibrated from end to end, spray coming over the high sides, as the river tried to take them.

He nodded to Faith.

She sawed at the rope and he saw the hemp strands snapping. Then the knife got through.

The boat bumped the bank once, and started to move. Freed from the rope, it came alive, quivering. The brown, foamy water sucked at it. The back—Shed's end—swung out into the stiffer current. He fought panic. The boat rocked, and then began to rotate end for end as the current began to get it more fully. Faith's end moved out faster than his, going first frontwards and then backwards, turning completely around twice, and they swung out into the mainstream. Something hard knocked against the side once and then was gone, the bank receded at an unbelievable rate, and they were leaving the ferry behind, were being swept out into the middle, were turning slowly around, end for end, out of control.

FIVE

Shed instantly saw the problem, and chilled from head to foot. The Buttermilk narrowed where it curved around a sheer rock wall just ahead. The water had to be very fast there, and it might hide snags. He had to get the boat under control—go around the corner prow forward, using his strength on his oar at the back as a tiller.

The boat, however, seemed to have ideas of its own. It seemed too heavy in the rushing water, and frighteningly low. The soupy river water bubbled less than six inches from the gunwales. Spray bit his face and arms, and he was slightly confused by the pinwheeling action as the craft went completely around and shot along backwards. At the far end of the boat, Faith clung to her paddle with one hand and the rail with the other; her hair had come loose and flew in the wind, and her eyes were white with fear. Between her and Shed, the children huddled almost out of sight on the soggy floor of the boat, the boys hanging onto the seat, Elizabeth limp between them in her blankets.

The river roar intensified as they swept on nearer the curve.

"We got to get turned around," Shed called to Faith.

Her face twisted. "What? What?"

"Turn it around! We got to—"

"I can't hear—" Words were torn away by the wind and rumble "—want me to do?"

They were racing downstream into the broad curve now, their speed worse. Shed could see the froth lashing the sheer rock walls on either side, and the silver spatter of waves disintegrating in the air. His nerve almost faltered.

"Frontwards!" he screamed at her. *"Got to get going frontwards!"*

Faith's lips moved, but no words came. The roar buried them.

Cursing, Shed dug his oar deep into the water on his right side. The force of the flow almost tore it from his hands, but the action had the desired effect, acting as a partial brake. The boat tried to come about. He paddled with all his might.

Seeing his actions, Faith tried to use her own oar. She put it in on the same side as his. The slow, sliding rotation stopped, and they started veering the other way again, more backwards.

"The other side!" Shed yelled. *"The other side!"*

She understood, swung the oar across the boat in slathers of water, dug in again. His own oar went deep in unison with hers, and the boat shuddered, swinging out broadside. For an instant he thought they were going around the curve that way, the worst of all. He oared again, frantically.

The boat swung on around, putting the whole world right side forward again. The current caught it and seemed to hold it. Shed yelled to ease off on the back oar. Faith did not hear, but she stopped then, because the current whipped them in closer to the rocks on the left side and then twisted them around the bend in a vicious motion that blurred vision and threatened to twist Shed's head off his shoulders.

They seemed to gush up and over a swell, rotate sickeningly, and then—suddenly—begin to slow. A little wave splashed over the side, icily drenching his legs. Gasping, he looked around.

They had made the bend and were beyond it. They could no longer see back to the ferry, or to anything else familiar. Rock walls shot straight up on both sides. They were in an ever-widening gorge through which the river rushed turgidly, with less ferocity because the way was broader. Here and there a wrecked tree had snagged in rocks along the sides, but the current had the boat locked in its center. They plunged along.

Shed got his breath. He realized that even the rumble was less awesome here, because the river's pace seemed less. Although they were streaking along faster than a horse could run, it seemed almost casual after the first moments away from the ferry.

Shed looked to Faith and the children again, seeing their fear. He felt a stab of pity for them.

"It's better now," he called. "Nothing to be skeert of."

"I thought we were—gone," Faith said huskily.

"Naw. No worry. You git very wet?"

She looked down at herself as if she had forgotten she had a body. Her dress was darkly drenched to the knees, but she had not gotten wet anywhere else except for a few heavy spatter marks here and there.

"See for the tykes," Shed suggested.

Putting her oar inside the boat, she crawled forward to the middle seat. She straightened Elizabeth up between the boys and parted the blankets to examine her face. Then she turned to Richard, soothed her hand through his wet hair, spoke softly to Jason.

"I was *scared!*" Jason chirped.

"We just had to get 'er under control," Shed called, dipping his oar lightly to correct a slight new tendency toward turning sideways against the current.

"Will there be many places like . . . back there?" Faith asked.

"Awyep," Shed said honestly. Then, seeing her dismay, he added quickly, "That might be the worst of 'em. You can't tell."

She looked at the rushing water and canyon walls. "We're going very fast."

"Faster we go, the faster we git there."

"I'm afraid."

"Nothin' to be afraid of now. Don't worry the tykes."

She eyed him. "Have we . . . done the right thing?"

"Too late to worry about it now."

Jason said brightly, "That river is *cold* when it splashes on you!"

"Most of it's melted snow, boy," Shed explained.

"And are we going *way* down in this boat?"

"Way down." Shed smiled, thinking that alone he knew how far it really was. If they knew, he thought, they would only be dismayed.

Faith clambered back to the far end, and braced herself on the seat. "The boat doesn't leak."

"She's a good boat," Shed agreed.

"Will we be able to stop when we want? Get out to eat or rest?"

"Awyep," he said, thinking, *If we're lucky.*

She stared again at the moving rock walls, then briefly toward the sky. The sky did not look good, Shed thought, and wondered if she had been in this country long enough to read sky even a little bit. If she read the signs of more rain or snow, and thought about the only effect it could have on the Buttermilk, she might act less calm.

Or maybe not. She had amazing control. She was so strong, he thought again, quietly surprised, as he always was when he confronted this. There were few men who would risk this trip on this river at this time, and perhaps no other women.

The boat trembled slightly, warning him.

He looked ahead.

There was another turn—a narrower one. It looked worse. The curve was a chaotic rainbow of spray and foam. Already he could hear its growl. It was just a few hundred yards ahead, and the current had the boat locked in its grasp, hurtling it forward ever faster.

White water. The worst sign: snags, hidden rocks, whirlpool currents.

The boat slowly swung around and turned insanely backwards again. Shed groaned and grabbed for his oar. *"Turn 'er! Turn 'er!"*

Their speed had rocketed higher, and if Faith heard his words, she showed no obvious sign. But she was doing some of the right things instinctively, digging in hard with the long oar on one side only, creating drag. She had learned fast. Shed stopped trying to communicate and concentrated on using his own oar on the opposite side to get the crazy boat turned properly again. *Why did it want to do this? Why couldn't it—*

But there was no time for thought. The boat, wallowing, slowly began to come around again. Then it caught abreast the flow and hung there as if tied. Towering walls of granite shot straight up on both sides, close now, and the water around the boat was all froth. Shed cursed and spun his oar, feeling it bite. The boat swung sickeningly and he got the oar on the opposite side just in time to correct the reverse yaw before it went too far. Icy water spewed over them.

For an instant he was blinded and thought he had lost it. Then there was a flash of brightness and they were out of the spray, going hellishly fast, the rock walls a blur, and they hit a great wave and were pitched high—and then *down* again. The boat's planks hit the water with a sound like hammers on rocks, and Shed was momentarily blinded again, and then he got an instant's free sight along the length of the crazy boat and he saw the boys *off the floor of the boat,* suspended in the air, just before the boat thrust up sharply again, catching them and sending them sprawling.

The little girl was going to get killed or thrown out right here and now, Shed thought. But he did not have time to speculate on it. There was another hump upward, a terrific crash, and then a slewing motion as the boat slammed out of control and sideways again through some kind of blurry vortex.

It was beginning to seem a nightmare. Shed's arms and back were afire with fatigue, already, yet he had no choice but to keep trying. He was drenched, and had little idea what he was doing. The work that year, long ago, made some of his movements automatic. He spun the oar overhead, trying repeatedly to catch the boat's turning. It came around once and he got a glimpse behind him, the way they had come. It was all an impossible hell of movement.

Rock cliffs raced past. The boat leaped high in the water again and slammed down hard, smashing him sideways into the rail. He felt a rib collapse, and the bright pain cut through the confusion. He lost all sense of what he *should* do, and began fighting his tormentor, the river.

The spray dropped away suddenly and he saw that they were going frontwards—Faith at the front, hanging on, soaked, the boys in the middle huddled down over Elizabeth—and they were all being carried at frightening speed down what seemed a long hill of water, very deep and very smooth and fast, toward more erupting foam just below. He tried to brace himself—to figure out what to do—but they hit with an unbelievable impact and vaulted through it before he knew what was happening. There was a brown blur and a new gush of cold, a sensation of vertigo, another crashing blow, and then simply more speed.

Shaking himself like a dog, Shed got things back into focus. They were all here—everybody still in the boat—and the cliff walls seemed to be racing away from them on both sides. Then he understood: the canyon walls were widening here, and, with a wider traverse, the river also seemed to be slowing, because its space was greater. Up ahead, the walls moved back even farther and he recognized the general area they were in, several miles downstream already from the ferry.

"Okay now!" he yelled at the family. *"Okay now!"*

The boat continued to race along, but after the rapids it seemed almost a normal pace. Shed took a deep breath and wiped water from his face and hair with his hand. He shot Faith an encouraging grin. They had made a bad place, he thought. She was frightened and hanging on with both hands, but they had made it—

Which was when it registered.

"*Where is it?*" he screamed at her.

She stared at him. Her lips moved, but the roar carried words away.

It was not necessary for him to hear the words. There was only one answer. Her oar was gone. In the very first encounter, the river had taken her oar from them.

Shed told himself it was not so bad. Rowing was hardly necessary anyway. The oars were good only for steering. Slumped in the front of the boat, Faith Slocumbe was already beaten, unable to summon strength for using an oar anyway. And he had known from the start that he was effectively alone against the Buttermilk.

Still the bitterness came. He had an impulse to get the boat to the bank, crawl out, and leave them. The chalky cliffs were steep all through this area—walls against the gray-cloudy sky far overhead. But he could climb out. He could leave them, get out while he still had life.

As quickly as he thought of it, however, he knew he wasn't going to do it. He had made a choice, stupid as it was. He could not climb out and walk away. He had started something and it had to be finished. If he could get them near Eagle Grove, he could leave them and strike out northwest. In only a day or two he could be back into more familiar territory, and capable of hiding himself from anyone who sought him.

Now, with the river carrying them toward Eagle Grove, every moment moved him closer to other men. He knew the danger they posed, whether anyone found out about Mashrow and Glass, back at the ferry, or not. But he couldn't think too much about that, either. The thing was to get the damned boat down the stream as quickly as possible, get near Eagle Grove, and get the hell out. The quicker the better.

Glancing at the tykes, he saw they were shivering. Then he saw that he was shivering, too. They had all been thoroughly soaked, and the speed down the river put them in a perpetual chill wind. They could not stop, however. It would take a long stop, and a trek for wood, and a big fire, to dry anything out. There was no time. If he had been right, and the Buttermilk was still on the rise, a delay could only make matters worse.

They had to keep going as long as they could.

The trip through the first white water had left an inch or two of muddy swamp sloshing in the deep bottom of the boat. This water splashed against Elizabeth's bundled form. Looking ahead and seeing no change in the course as far as the next big bend, Shed gestured toward the bundle and indicated that Faith could crawl back and check on the little girl.

She crawled awkwardly in the bottom water, petted each of the boys for a moment, and picked up the soggy bundle. She unwrapped it carefully, fear carving deep lines in her face. She looked, her eyes dilated. Then she hugged the bundle close to her and began a little instinctive rocking motion.

Shed breathed again. Elizabeth was alive.

Using his oar as a tiller, he maintained the boat's position in the center of the stream. Rushing along with them in the water was all manner of debris: tree limbs, planks, chunks of matted vegetation, and whole bushes and small trees. One particularly large tree trunk swept along beside the boat for some time, then suddenly snagged on something hidden, erupted into a geyser of foam, and fell behind the boat at an astonishing rate. It showed how really fast the boat was carrying them along.

It began to rain.

"Sorry!" Shed yelled to the family. "Just have to git wet!"

No one smiled or got the joke. They stared at him.

Shed realized what a sorry, bedraggled pack they all were. "Never said it'd be easy."

Although the river flowed slower than before, conversation was still difficult, having to be conducted in shouts. There was nothing to say anyway. Shed kept his eyes on the river, fearfully watching for half-hidden rocks or other snags.

For a while longer, however, the river seemed to relent. It twisted broadly between humpy mountains that stood high above them, but there were no bad narrows. The rain continued to come down, warmer than the river water. It actually began to feel good, steady and soothing, pelting on his back and shoulders.

As time slipped by, Shed saw the terrain slowly changing, becoming more rugged. They were moving into the deeper canyons. Now, he seldom saw good banks along the sides for a quick landing, and this worried him, so he began watching more nervously for the places that did appear. Often, rock walls fell straight into the river on either side; if something happened here, there would be no place to beach the boat or climb out: they would be swept downstream like the logs and branches.

The thought banished Shed's fragile sense of security. They had been in the boat a long time now. He did not know how long, exactly, because he could not see the sun, but he thought it was now late morning. He was hungry, and had begun to ache all over. Somewhere along the line he had barked a fingertip, and the bloody nail hung backward by a thread of pink flesh. When the water hit the wound, it stung and throbbed. If he got out of this with no worse injury, he thought, he would be more than just lucky.

He felt, however, that he had at least begun to understand the boat. He no longer trembled inside every time the craft sloshed from side to side. It was big and it was heavy, and although it seemed unstable in the water, responding to every movement, it did not tip far. The way it rode low was frightening, but kept it from being more tipsy. Perhaps, Shed thought, it was like a tree that bent easily so it would not break.

He congratulated himself on this insight, and felt better again.

"Where do you think we are?" Faith called to him after a while.

"Don't know," Shed replied. "A far piece, I'd say, from Bung's."

"Are we making better time than you expected?"

"Can't say," he said, seeing that she was groping for a reassurance that he could not give. "We're going fast, but there's a long ways to go yet—mighty long ways."

"Do you know about where we are?"

"I been all along this river on foot. Hard to recognize things, the water so high and all."

"But we're making good time?"

For just an instant, he was wildly angry with her. *God damn you,* he wanted to shout, *I'm taking you down this river. I'm fighting this Buttermilk for you. Don't ask any more of me. Don't expect me to make it any easier for you, because I can't, I ain't God.*

But the rage vanished as swiftly as it rose. Looking at her, seeing the desperate hope in her eyes, he saw that her weakness—the need for reassurance—was not really her fault. Everybody looked to something else or someone else for this kind of support. He always took it from the land and the weather and his skills. She, being a woman, had to take strength from him.

Well, that was all right. He had enough strength. He had plenty for the world, if need be. Sometimes he dreamed he was a giant, striding over towns, stepping over mountains, all-powerful, all-knowing, impervious to everything. He always awoke from these strange dreams feeling good, and powerful, as he had when asleep. And he *was* strong. If she needed to lean on him, he was plenty strong enough.

"We're makin' good time," he reassured her.

Her eyes gladdened faintly. "Do you think we're past the worst places?"

He knew they weren't, but he was started now. "Might be," he lied. "Might not be, too. Can't tell. We been through enough, though, right?"

A touch of color appeared in her face, and animation showed behind her eyes. In a second, she was quite amazingly transformed. She sat up straighter, drawing encouragement from his words.

It was a strange moment for Shed. He watched her

and was softly startled. *Look at her!* he thought. *Look at the power I got over her!*

He was not merely taking these people down the river in a physical sense, he thought suddenly. He was carrying them on his back, as far as their spirits were concerned. He had started with them and he was the strongest and therefore he was *responsible.*

Shed saw this very vaguely, but he saw it: to succeed, he had to do more than carry their bodies to Eagle Grove. He had to keep them hoping, keep them in good spirits. A thing that lost its spirit soon died. He had seen it with injured deer many times, and even, once, with a panther. The panther had been caught in some fool's trap, and tore its right front paw half off to get away. This had taken courage and strength, things Shed could admire. But then the panther had crawled into a cave and sulked. As badly hurt as it was, it might have survived, because after a while its bleeding stopped. But it did not make any attempt to eat, even after Shed had found it and become interested and tossed down meat for it. The panther, it seemed, had understood the extent of its injury, had looked ahead to a life as a cripple, and had just given up. Without caring, it simply died.

The woman and the children could be like the panther, Shed saw now. The trip had been tough so far, and it was going to get worse—much worse. The river might break them unless he could keep them going. They might just give up. He had to keep them from giving up.

This was a very grave responsibility, he thought. He wondered if he could handle it. He had never been around people that much. Most of his knowledge of them was from his childhood, and that was a long time ago now. Most people he'd known were vague memories.

He remembered a mother, though. He could not remember what she had looked like. But she had been soft and warm and very grave and tender. His memories of her were all pink and fluffy and sweet-smelling, and her voice had been like music. She had gone away when he was little. He could remember the aching void after she was gone. Had she died? He thought so. But the spells had come more often upon him as a child, and he remembered mostly the terror of them, how they hurt, the way he felt when they were over and he knew he had had one and everybody looked at him soberly, watching to see if he was mad.

They had thought he was mad at school, back there in Hannibal. He remembered trying—ah, God, the way he had *tried!*—to learn to read and cipher. But the words always got mixed up, going in crazy directions in his head, and he couldn't make them come out straight. He could still, right this instant, feel *everything* about all those times at school: the hunched-over pain between his shoulder blades, the cold metal rail of the desk against his bare leg as he strained over the damned little book, staring, trying to focus and *make* the words go in straight lines, and the smell of dust and oil on the floor, and chalk dust, and the dry heat from the stove in the winter, and always the sniggering behind him—Toby Bacter, or Rufus Cline, or Mary Anne Oliphant.

Remembering, he shriveled inside.

But he had made it, he reminded himself. He was his own man. He needed nothing from anybody. He was a *man.* And now here he was, with these people needing *him.* –How many of those bastards back in Hannibal would have been able to get this boat and do what he had already done? How many of *them* understood why a deer, or a panther sometimes, might just lie down and die? He needed nothing from anybody. He was stronger than anybody. He stood alone. He *did* tower over towns and mountains, just like in his dreams. He was–

"Mister Shed!"

The woman's words were soft but sharp, drawing him back to reality. He looked up and saw the fright in her eyes. He wondered if he had had a small spell or something.

They were still moving along in the mainstream, but the stream was faster. The rock walls of the canyon here were jagged, narrower. The boat had begun to vibrate softly from end to end, almost as if it were singing.

Faith pointed ahead.

Shed balanced his oar across his knees and licked his lips, tasting the grit of the river. He looked where she pointed.

There was a narrows. The river, crushed into a quarter of its swollen width between the rock walls, seemed to rise up into one continuous explosion. There were rocks there, some bigger than a house, and spray a hundred feet in the air, debris being caught, crushed, thrown upward.

Shed went cold as the boat picked up speed, hurtling toward its destruction. He thought about giving up, putting his hands over his head to protect himself as in a fall. But then he caught a glimpse of something through the spray. The left side of the channel was not as bad as the right. The water seemed to gush through cleanly on the far side, going insanely fast, but without boils or eruptions. *Deeper water—smoother water.*

On the right, an entire tree exploded out of the river, crashed against the hidden rocks, and began to break up. It was less than a hundred yards ahead. The boys were sitting up high in the middle now, looking at the chaos with wide, frightened eyes. Faith, clinging to the boat with one hand, was trying feebly to call something to him over the roar.

Shed saw this in an instant, but was already taking action of his own. If there was a chance, it was to the left. He swung his oar and dug deep, contesting the force of the river with an effort that sent shock waves up his spine.

The boat veered sharply in the direction he wanted it to go. It tried to swing on around broadside, but he was clever about the things the boat liked to do now, and stopped it. They were almost into the rapids. Over the din, he heard Faith scream. He had no time to look at her. The boat was trying to go into the worst rapids, bucking like a wild horse, but he stopped it and got it turning the other way, toward the safer side, and then the boat obeyed and shot off in that direction, throwing him to the bottom. He hit face first, tasting blood, struggled back up, the oar still in his hand. He got onto the seat again, half blinded. Things shot past on both sides. The tree was near. He couldn't hear anything. Branches tore at the side planks, making a noise like another scream. The boat went up, lurching, and over a crest, and fell out from under him. It hit in a gigantic spray and went right on, and then suddenly they were beyond the worst of it, shooting out into frothy water like a shot from a gun, plunging along in foamy waves, the river widening faster already, pitching but not out of control.

All were still where they were supposed to be. They had all gotten drenched again. Dazed, they stared at Shed. He spat out a tooth and some blood and grinned at them. Ahead it was calmer again.

SIX

Having tried for the second time to kill them, the Buttermilk subsided again. It wound sluggishly into a long, broad valley, where it could spread out over vast, grassy fields. It sent tendrils out into woods and gullies, uprooting a tree here, bringing out chunks of brush and dead vegetation there. The canyon country seemed to have vanished.

The rain eased off; the air was colder and flecks of snow appeared in it.

Shed kept *Death* in the center of the stream. The boat glided along imperturbably, not much faster than a man might trot. Shuddering from the cold and soaked to the skin, Shed probed around in his mouth and found that he had lost one front tooth and two others were loose. He occupied himself for a while by working at the loose ones with his fingers, but this hurt too much and he quit, telling himself they might tighten up again. He would be able to eat around them and they would be little trouble unless they got infected.

Gray, her face stretched taut by discomfort and tension, Faith watched him in silence a while, studied the passing country with its mud, water, and patches of melting snow, and then busied herself trying to help the children. She struggled with the knots on Shed's packs for a while but could not get them open. Shed, irritated because she chose to eat without asking permission, did not help her. Finally she gave up and tended to Elizabeth, rocking her awhile. Then she spoke softly to the boys.

Jason listened for a while, then looked up toward Shed's end of the boat. "Is it true?" he piped.

"Is what true?" Shed countered.

"Are we going right on till it's dark, and not stop?"

Shed exchanged glances with Faith. "Is that what she said?"

"She said we might."

"Well, she's right. We might."

"I'm hungry. Are you hungry?"

"Awyep."

"Why don't we stop and eat, then?"

"Because I said."

Jason considered. "My paw always said you ought to give a reason."

"I ain't your paw, boy."

"*I* know that."

"Then don't talk foolish."

"I only meant, if you're hungry, and we're hungry, why don't we–"

"Because *I said*, and there's an end to it!"

Jason's forehead wrinkled and his mouth puckered up.

"And don't give me no sulky looks!" Shed told him.

"He's getting tired," Faith interjected.

"I'm getting tired, too," Shed told her. "We're all getting tired. Why don't you try to be like the other cub, there? You don't hear *him* complaining, asking fool questions."

Faith touched her mute son's soggy hair, pushing it back off his forehead with infinite care. "He can't talk. You know that."

"Maybe he can," Shed said, "and maybe he can't."

"I told you he can't. He never has. He doesn't understand half of what's going on, the poor thing, and—"

"You don't know that," Shed snapped.

"What?" she faltered.

"You don't know he can't talk," Shed told her. "Maybe he just don't want to talk yet."

"I wish that were true."

Jason said, "He really can't talk, mister."

"Look at him," Shed said. "Taking it all in. Watching us all the time. Maybe you think he's dumb, but I don't. Nope. I sure don't. He probably could talk iffen he wanted." He grinned at Richard. "Only why bother, right, boy? Right?"

Richard frowned and passed a chubby hand across his face, as he did sometimes, as if to brush away cobwebs.

"See?" Shed demanded.

Faith, her own frown deepening watched him in silence, as if trying to understand him and his moods. Her silence began to infuriate him.

"Quit looking at me like that!"

"I bet," Jason said bravely, "you'd not be so cranky if we ate."

Shed had to grin at him. "I'll say one thing, boy. You got enough spunk."

Jason grinned back at him tentatively.

"You skeert of me?" Shed demanded.

"Yes sir," Jason said.

"Damn right!" Shed chortled. "You better be! I'm the

man that's taken on the Buttermilk, right? I'm the man that's taken on the job of gettin' you to Eagle Grove, right? You got good sense to be skeert. People oughtta be skeert of me. You remember it!" Then, seeing Jason's bright eyes, he softened. "You want to come back here and sit up here on the seat with me?"

Jason started to move. Faith caught his arm. "No."

"All right, then, and damn the lot of you! Stay where you are. Hunker down there in the water, for all I care, and be damned."

He did not understand his mood swings with these people. They made him furious one instant and all soft and squishy inside the next. It was infuriating. He had intended to stop in this broad valley somewhere, tie up, and eat. He badly needed a brief rest and the energy of food. Now he decided to push on.

Little by little, the valley began to narrow. Rock outcroppings appeared after another hour or so. The snow vanished from the air and the sky grew brighter, and then grayer again, and a warm wind began to blow and the rain came back, obscuring the world. The rain felt warm, pounding on Shed's back at first, but after a while it seemed to get colder. Bitterly he steered the boat past the last outcropping that might have made a good place for stopping, and then the river was back in its stone channel again, moving faster, the wind brittle and biting against his face and wet clothing.

Shed began to doubt the wisdom of his actions. He knew generally where they were, and unless he missed his guess, they would soon be into a long string of deep gorges where there would be no chance at all to beach the boat or tie up for a rest. Inwardly he cursed himself for letting *them* change his decision.

After what seemed a long time, the rain was worse and they came upon a place where the river split around a rocky outcropping that had a small, muddy beach and a few trees standing high. Shed watched the island approach. He was dull from fatigue. It was deep afternoon. He decided he had taught the family its lesson, and steered the boat toward the shale beach.

Feeling clever, he swung the boat around at the last moment so he could hop out first, on pain-pricky legs, and drag the boat farther aground.

It was a bare place, eroded dirt and rock, everything soaked in mud, and the trees well back, and the raw wind beating the rain into them. The boys and Faith Slocumbe sat in the boat as if stunned. Furious for no reason, Shed pulled the boat further up on the embankment, using a bone-wrenching effort.

He signaled to them. "Get out. Stretch. Rest. Eat."

The boys climbed out stiffly, hobbling in the mud and then standing there like little muddy statues. Faith tried to climb out with her burden of the little girl, staggered, and would have fallen back into the boat if Shed had not caught her under the arm. He helped her out.

"We'll rest a while," he yelled at her over the din of the rain and the river. "Food! Try to warm up!"

Faith held Elizabeth close against her. "She's so sick. So hot!"

Shed turned away from her, because he could not face her. Dragging his larger pack out of the boat, he angrily dumped the contents onto a wet, flat rock. Then, taking his knife, he ripped the pack along the seams, making of it a large, irregularly shaped chunk of canvas. He motioned for the tykes to sit down and they obeyed. He gestured to Faith. She slumped to the wet ground, close by the boys. Shed draped the canvas over and around them, snuggling it under their legs and feet and leaving only a little breathing loop in front of their faces. The canvas was wet, but the rain streamed off its hard surface. Inside it, even wet, they would begin to warm up. Their body heat would make it like a soggy tent, snug after a little while.

He tried not to notice that the boys' lips were blue.

Lightning crackled overhead, thunder crashed against rock walls, reverberating, and the rain intensified. Shed went through the contents of the destroyed pack, jamming some things into pockets. He handed the family some soggy strips of dried meat and a cloth-wrapped package of cold cooked potatoes they had brought along. They sat under the canvas and chewed at the stuff, watching him with great eyes.

To show his nonchalance, he squatted on his heels in front of them, grinned, and tore a chunk off another strip of meat, eating lustily.

Faith moved the flap of the canvas cover.

"Don't!" he said sharply.

"Get inside with us!" she urged.

"Hell no!"

"It's warmer."

"I know that."

"Get in, then."

"Don't need it."

"You want us to think you're warm enough just like that?"

"Awyep."

She stared at him, uncomprehending. He tore off another chunk of meat and chewed it with signs of great relish.

He was getting very tired, and he knew it was a hell of a mess. He had begun to gain confidence, however, that he might get them through it if they believed in him. People were like that. They could do more than they thought they could do, if they believed in someone or something. He was not a very good thing to believe in, but he was all they had. He could push them harder as long as they were fooled and thought he was really all right.

But behind his mask of confidence he was still badly shaken. The Buttermilk definitely was continuing to rise. He had never traversed all the country between this position and Eagle Grove, but he knew some of the river still ahead. There was at least one falls. He had to watch out for that falls and possibly others like it.

There were too many other things to watch out for, also. From about this point, the Buttermilk cut through bigger canyons. *Death*—the boat—had not been constructed with high sides and the stoutest oak planks for no reason. At the best and calmest of seasons, the river held peril between here and the town. There were places, it was said, that could turn a man's hair white.

Shed hated it. All of it. He hated the river, the cold and wet, the rain, the roaring sounds, the hidden rocks and logs and whirlpools and falls and the boat. Most of all, he felt a deep loathing for the way the family watched him, humbly, trusting.

No one had ever trusted him before. It was a very

strange and frightening feeling. He came back to his earlier thought: It was as if he were literally carrying them all on his back. He not only had to make all the right moves, he had to make them continue to believe in him. And how could a man do this when his guts were curdled and sour with sheer terror?

Well, he told himself, he was not that afraid.

But he could not fool *himself*, too. That was just too much to ask.

"You're cold, too," Faith told him now.

"No," he grunted.

"You're shaking."

"Shaking makes you warmer. Shaking is good."

"If you get under the cover with us—"

"Don't boss me, woman, God damn it!"

She recoiled and pulled the canvas closer.

Jason piped up. "Is it much farther?"

"Some," Shed told him, softening.

"Will we be there in an hour?"

"Not likely, boy."

"*Two* hours?"

"Tomorrow, maybe."

Faith said, "You told me it would be longer."

"Do you *want* it to be longer?"

"Of course not. I—"

"Well, then, don't argue with me!"

She subsided, hurt and bewildered.

Hell, Shed thought. "The river's takin' us faster than I thought. We oughtta get there tomorrow. Late maybe."

She nodded.

"Can you hold out?" Shed asked her.

She looked surprised. "Of course."

Yes, he thought. She could hold out. Jesus, she was so strong. She could hold out. The river might tear the boat to splinters and break their bones, but she would hold out. Nothing could touch her. If he had had a woman like her twenty years ago—

Surprised by the thought, he quickly walked around it.

The rain showed no signs of easing. It was tempting to remain at this spot longer. Despite the cold, Shed hunkered on his heels in the mud and closed his eyes and let the rain drum against him. He dozed. Random thoughts flicked through his mind, and once there was a dark blank. He had a dream in which he was a bear, and walked late in the afternoon in a cold place, looking for a cave or a big tree hollowed out. He *felt* like a bear in the dream, and it was all right, being a bear, except that he remembered once being a man. Then he dreamed he was walking, as a bear, down a hill toward a pond where water was running, and he started to fall and he woke up with a start, because he had almost toppled off his heels in the mud.

He looked at his family. Faith held the little girl close, but her eyes were closed as if she were dozing. Jason's head was on his chest. Richard was staring at Shed with bright, vacant eyes.

"Y'all right, boy?" Shed asked softly.

Richard showed nothing.

"You're fine," Shed told him.

Richard blinked.

"Of course y'are," Shed said.

The rain continued to beat down. Shed got to his feet on legs that felt like they were on fire, from the squatting so long. He walked around in the slippery mud, getting his circulation back. He went to the bank and, back to the others, urinated into the river.

He thought, This is for you, Buttermilk. You're not getting us this trip.

The thought amused him and he felt better. The river had tested him and he had won. There might be worse ahead, but he was more clever now, and ready. He was not quite so afraid. He would get through regardless of the Buttermilk's evil intent, because he was smarter than any river, and stronger. He had not lived in nature all these years for nothing. It had all been getting ready for this test, and he had been more ready than he had realized. He felt almost eager to get back on the water and let the river do its damndest.

"Let's go, let's go," he said to his family.

He got them into the boat. The canvas made a fairly good cover for Faith and Elizabeth in the front, and he gave the tykes his jacket. They huddled under it on the boat's floor boards. He shoved *Death* off the bank and hopped in, making the vessel squish this way and that, dangerously. But he knew what he was doing now and there was no problem. He dug in his oar and sent the boat skimming heavily out into the main current. The main current took *Death* and turned her, and swept her rapidly along past the island.

The rain began to ease up as they reached the channel and accelerated. The gray, muddy water was now pocked by raindrops only every now and then, and it was possible to see ahead, where great cliffs rose up to line the river. At a distance, the river looked like a yellow ribbon in a darker-colored vee, and beyond that point there were taller hills and mountains, and Shed knew the river went past all of them.

The river picked up speed and plunged into the vee.

Shed worked his oar expertly, holding the boat dead into the center. It held course well and had a solidity about it that was reassuring. He had begun to feel a certain affection for the boat, as he felt for the river itself. They were all comrades, he thought, and there was nothing they had to fight about.

The river continued to pick up speed. Now, although it was a swollen hundred yards wide between sheer granite cliffs, and very deep, there were whorls here and there in the surface throwing up chilly spray. When the boat slapped into one of the whorls, it tried to turn but was through before much turning could be done. Then Shed straightened things out again.

The course bent sharply to the left, and then back to the right, then left again. It narrowed slightly, foaming. The roaring sound increased. Shed worked his oar, his side hurting from the effort and his breath coming hard. He noticed fleetingly that everyone was holding to the sides again, and the tykes' coat-cover had fallen to the bottom of the boat.

Even as the speed continued to increase and Shed struggled to keep things in a straight line, he reflected that the furious pace was not all bad unless things worsened considerably. He was very tired now. The hours of fighting had worn him worse than he could have anticipated, and his gritty, soaked clothing had chafed his skin raw in a dozen places. But they were making fantastic time; it could be nothing like three days down to

Eagle Grove if the river continued carrying them this swiftly.

Possibly the family saw this, he thought. They were plainly scared, but had done no complaining since the rest stop.

He had expected crying, at least, some measure of terror. Even the little ones had maintained a composure that baffled him. Faith, despite the constant battering of water and wind and fear, still managed to sit upright, her chin thrust forward as if she were daring the river to do worse.

Ah, God, they were all strong. Like her, they were strong.

Shed had never known people like them.

Fleetingly, he wondered where they had come from. He knew very little about them. Now he had begun to want to know more. You did not share an experience like this, over many hours, without feeling this way, he thought. Whether they liked it or not, the river had pressed them together. None of them would ever be quite the same again.

He wanted to reassure the family.

"*Be all right!*" he yelled at them over the growing roar. He gave them a grin that he hoped looked brighter than he really felt.

Bracing his knees inside the gunwales on the seat, he leaned on the long oar, tillering the boat along the rushing current. He was aware that he had no banks on either side, if something happened, but he couldn't take time to look very carefully.

He was very busy with the river by this time. He had never gone this fast in his life. He had no idea how fast the river was taking them, but the pace was still quickening. The cliffs on either side were not so tall now, but he could see that they were in the depths of a monstrous canyon, stretching out craggy rock formations and chimneys of stone as far on either side as his eye could see. It was as if they had reached the bottom of the world, and he couldn't hear himself think. Testing, he shouted. Except for the vibration inside his skull, it was as if he hadn't even tried to make a sound.

The river was now flowing downhill at such a slope that he could see it.

His earlier confidence began to slide away with the speed of the mad river. It was beginning to be very serious. He did not know what was ahead, but the river was now carrying *Death* at a pace that made the wind rush wet against his face and flap his shirt. The rock walls on either side were blurry when viewed with an eye toward any detail. He saw some kind of animal—a deer or an elk—churn, tumbling along in the current abreast of the boat. The animal was dead, and it was being carried along so swiftly it did not have time to sink. It was too broken to identify.

There was a terrible impersonality to this river, and its power was so great that Shed had no time to think about it. Ahead was white water—how much or how serious, he could not tell. There was absolutely no question of getting to the bank; his oar, when it bit the current, was as if it were encased in hands of steel. Spray broke over the front, dousing him in ice again, and he caught a glimpse of his family huddling against the sides of the boat, and then the white water was just ahead.

Death hit the tornadic water activity nose down, leaped

as if stung, and dropped sickeningly through the air before crashing to the surface with an impact that sizzled up Shed's spine. He had an instant's glimpse of great, wet rocks—brown-froth rocks like houses—on either side. Then he saw several shattered boulders in the water just ahead, and shouted again, this time from fear, and dug in the oar as deeply and hard as he could, tearing things in his side. The boat swung slightly, somehow got past the rocks, leaped a little waterfall, swung sideways, went up and then down a long, swirling cascade, swung around again. He caught it the second time around and got it going straight long enough to miss a huge rock formation. Then the water seemed to rise straight up—obscuring everything ahead—and the boat soared up—*up!*—and broke out on the top and slid over on its side, yawing insanely, and *this* time when the crash came, Shed felt the shocking impact of rocks.

He was drenched, blinded, hanging on with the oar, knowing that any moment was the last.

The boat was damaged. It might be finished. Something in his left arm was hurt badly.

Solid water smashed against his body, receded, smashed him again. He had the sensation of going up and up and then down on the far side, like it had been when he slid down hills, in the winter, on a sled, as a child. But that had been controllable, and the fear, although real, something only to be tested and endured for the fun of having known it. *This* was—my God, *more* boulders, and the boat somehow racing past them, the front swinging to the left to miss one, the back swinging the other direction to miss another, and he was making some of it happen, how much he didn't know.

And then, all at once, the boat shot out of the foam and into surging water without spray.

Gasping, Shed saw more spray ahead. Great, barrel-shaped rock formations, church formations and nightmare formations, were on all sides, and the sky was a gray patch far, far away, between the rock formations, as if at the end of a gigantic corridor. Then *Death* was back into torment again.

Shed did not know how much more the boat could take. He did not know how much more he could take. He was past endurance or thinking. Water came over him in a solid wall, battering with the force of a wild beast. He was blinded again, could not get his breath, lost all sense of direction. His vision was through torrents of mud. Then he could not see at all. He fought with everything he had, trying by blind feel alone to keep himself upright, and the boat turned to what *felt* the right direction. The roar had deafened him again and his hearing simply stopped, so that there was only a strange ringing in his head. He felt oddly detached from himself, seemed to observe his own beating. The boat writhed, pitched, battered him, and he had no idea what was going on, but he knew they were lost, were probably already under the surface somewhere. But then the boat pitched high upward, as if shaking its head in defiance, and for an instant he saw sky and could breathe.

There was a shocking impact that hurled him to the floor of the boat. He climbed back up to the seat in time to lose his breath as a huge wave covered him with a force that felt like it might peel his flesh. He was screaming at the river but did not know what he was saying.

It went on.

The boat lurched out of a kind of whirlpool, broke out of spray, and rocked violently as it reached more placid water. After all the pitching, the straightforward movement of the boat felt like acceleration, and Shed felt a stab of terror that there was even more just ahead. Clawing at his eyes, he got a gritty view ahead—off the side of the pinwheeling craft—and saw a widening, a calming.

He took a shuddering breath.

At that instant, Faith screamed.

It was a terrible sound, splitting all the other tumult, and Shed swung around on the seat to face her.

She was on her feet, her hands in her wild-flowing hair, and she was staring at the center section of the boat with a look of horror that Shed could not believe.

In the middle of the boat, boards on the left side had been smashed, broken inward. Water gushed in. Elizabeth, bundled on the floor, was half under water. Richard, clearly terrified, was scrambling around and around beside her, making little moaning sounds and grasping at the air, as if he thought he could catch something.

Jason was gone.

SEVEN

The night was a vast black, with no moon or stars. The rain had gone away, and all around the little camp, towering in the darkness, were gigantic rocks and monuments. Thirty feet from the smoky campfire was the Buttermilk, invisible, its nearby gurgling overlaid by the ominous roar of its passage through the gorge. Shed sat on one side of the little fire, huddling close for warmth and light. The remaining boy, Richard, slept under the crook of Shed's arm. Across the fire, Faith held Elizabeth close, swathed in the blankets. Faith rocked her with a terrible regularity, forward and backward on her buttocks.

Shed had never in his life been so tired.

He had no idea how far they had come. He was not sure it mattered. They probably had as far to go. He knew sleep would help him partially recover so he could go on; his ribs burned, and it hurt to breathe deeply, and he thought something was broken in his left arm, because he could not move it without agony, and his mouth was swollen and raw where his teeth had been smashed; still, he could go on.

But Faith, rocking, silent, terrified him.

He had seen women like this. Once after a terrible fire

in Hannibal. Once after a multiple killing near St. Louis. Once on a wagon train, after an Indian massacre.

Mad.

She could *not* go mad. He had to get her out of it some way.

He tried to catch her glazed, unseeing eyes with his own. "Is the girl all right?" he asked.

Faith kept rocking. Back and forth. Back and forth.

"The girl," Shed said. "Is she all right?"

"Yes," Faith said finally in an absolutely dead voice.

"Try an' git her to eat."

There was no response.

"Try an'—"

"She won't."

"Try."

For an instant her eyes locked on him. "I did. She won't."

"Is the fever—?"

"Back."

Shed accepted the news with hidden bitterness. It was all the wind and water and pitching around in the boat all day; that was what had done it. The medicine should have kept the fever down longer than this. It was a very bad sign.

Faith rocked.

Shed tried again to jar her out of it. "You eat, then," he said.

She rocked.

"I said, *you* better eat."

She rocked.

"He's gone," Shed said. "The boy is gone. You got to try to git used to it. I know it's hard. Nothing will make it no easier. Nothing going to change it. The boat hit a rock and busted and he tumbled out and he's *gone*. Ain't no bringing him back. —You hear me?"

Faith Slocumbe continued to rock. Her face was smooth, incredibly tired and filled with pain, yet with a majesty about it. She had withdrawn inside her face. She was—almost—no longer there.

"Damn it!" Shed said loudly. "Talk!"

She turned and seemed to recognize him again. Her face remained eerily placid. "He was my first-born."

"I *know* that," Shed groaned. "But *you* got to keep living. That's what you do. You keep on living. You don't quit."

"Leave me be."

Shed sighed.

He knew he could not expect better from her. The shock had been almost too much for him, too, and he had long ago learned to be ready for anything. One minute Jason had been there, hanging on, and the next—he had simply been gone. If there had been a scream . . . or a glimpse of him being carried overboard perhaps . . . *something*—it might not have been quite so bad.

Shed had battled the damaged boat to the shore, and they had gotten out, run up and down the narrow bank, trying vainly to catch sight of a small boy in the swirling water. There had been no sign. Faith had been screaming all the time. In her anguish, then, she had tried to run into the river, her arms outstretched, as if she could somehow *hug Jason out of the current*. Shed had narrowly caught her before she too was swept away. She had fought him, crying, struggling much harder than she had during those times he had taken her by force. Finally he had hit her, and she'd collapsed in a heap.

Later, nailing the boards of the boat back together as best he could with a rock for a hammer, Shed had explained that they could not stay here, that they had to go on. He was badly shaken at the time, and made what was for him a very long speech about accomplishing nothing by staying on the spot. He was even eloquent. He made the speech, and heard that it made no sense, not really, not in the face of Jason being *gone*.

But they had gotten back into the boat and gone on, and he was very busy all the remaining daylight hours, although the river had seemed to relent a little, having been given its sacrifice, and the way was not quite so bad.

Now, in the night, Shed faced her madness.

With his own first shock gone, the truth of it was that he felt more irritation and anger than real grief. He had known some of them might not make it. He expected Elizabeth to die at any time. Jason might also have been predicted. Shed had seen so much death. Everything died. Jason had gone early. A lot of people and things went early. It was bad but it could be accepted.

The woman was the one he had to save.

The woman and Richard. Because Elizabeth was dying.

Shed looked down at Richard. He hugged him under the heavy, wet coat from which steam was rising as the heat of the fire did its work.

Shed told him, "Your bud had bad luck, boy."

Richard blinked.

"Awyep," Shed grunted. "Bad luck. But that don't mean you'll have bad luck. You're gonna have good luck, you savvy? You're my buddy. You're my old partner, right? You and me. We get along. Right? You don't need to worry yourself. I got you through today. I'll get you through tomorrow. I'm taking you and your momma to Eagle Grove." Shed gave him another squeeze.

Richard put his thumb in his mouth and leaned his face against Shed's chest and closed his eyes for sleep.

"You sleep." Shed smiled. "Sure. Nobody going to hurt you. Not while they got John Riley Shed to fight. *I'm* your bud now."

The little boy cuddled closer. His body was warm and soft against Shed's. It was a very strange sensation, another body so close.

Shed felt better because of it. He would get Richard through, all right, he thought. Nothing would interfere with that. Richard and Faith. *Nothing* would interfere with that.

There had been more things he had wanted to tell Richard, about his own brother getting killed that time, and about other kids and school and how to cope with cruelty. But Richard was asleep already now, and Shed did not want to disturb him. There would be other days to tell it anyway. Maybe there would be many other days.

Gently, he slipped Richard away from him and wrapped him carefully in the heavy, steaming coat. Then, getting up with caution, he moved around the fire. He bent over Faith and the little girl. He parted the blanket to check on the little girl. She was afire, and her breath had a rotten odor.

"I'll hold her a while," Shed offered.

"No."

Faith had stopped rocking.

Shed went back to his own side of the fire.

At another time, he thought, or with different luck, it could have been a good night. He could have waited for the tykes to bed down, and then he could have quietly taken the woman again, beating into her to show her how much a man he was, even after such a day. She might have responded—not just tried to help, or be nice, but actually *responded*. Then she might have been different in the morning, almost happy, and they could have gone on. He might have told them a bear story to make them laugh.

Shed sighed.

He thought they might reach the vicinity of Eagle Grove by late tomorrow. He was no longer sure he could simply leave them there and walk away. But the alternatives were foggy in his mind, and unpleasant. He knew he could not actually go into Eagle Grove, because there were sure to be people there who would recognize him. He could not fight the whole town. He could fight anyone, one at a time. But he could not take on the whole town.

There was law in Eagle Grove, too. The law would want him . . . would give its blessing to anyone who tried to hurt him or kill him or drive him away. The law was an enemy, had always been an enemy. Since he was a child and the marshal had beaten him up for operating snares to try to catch beaver for the pelts and the money, the law had always been after him. The law was for normal people. The law was against people with damage to the brain.

So he could not go into Eagle Grove. Better to just walk

off a cliff or give himself to the Buttermilk. There was no going into any organized town in this part of the country.

He did not mind, he told himself. He would not know how to act with other people in a town anyway. Towns did things to people: made them nasty and hateful, closed-in. He did not mind having always to stay away from them, hiding.

But Faith had to go into Eagle Grove. And what he had to do was think of a way to be nice to her and explain to her that he *cared* now, and wanted her to come somewhere else—meet him—when the sickness was over. He wanted her along. For a long time.

The idea astonished him, but he could not deny it.

He wondered how he could say it to her so it would sound right. It was time for a regular woman. There were still places a man could go, and change his name and everything else, and start again.

Just her and him and Richard and Elizabeth . . . Elizabeth if she lived.

Shed watched her, yearning for this.

He was struck by a terrible loneliness, which was very odd, because he was seldom lonesome when he was alone. Did he *need* this woman?

He licked cracked lips. "I'm going to get us through," he told her.

She paid no attention.

"I know what you think about me," Shed told her. "Just a dumb, bad-smelling mountain man, right? Right. But I'll tell you what. I'm going to get us through. Ain't nothing else going to happen."

She rocked.

"A man can take just so much," Shed told her. "I've already had my share of bad luck in this life. My luck is turning good. This here Buttermilk can't do nothing more to me. We lost . . . the boy. But we got this here boy left. You think he's dumb? He ain't dumb. I know his kind. He's like me. People said I was dumb, once. I showed 'em. I make my own way. I stand on my own two feet. Nobody bosses me. Nobody makes me do *anything*. I ain't as bad as you think. I'm a *man*, you hear me? Nothing stops me, you hear me? I feel bad about little old Jason, too. Hell. I–" And suddenly he was shocked because his chest heaved and a great sob burst out of him.

He turned, horribly embarrassed, and stumbled out of the light of the fire.

What was going on here? Was he *crying?* All the things he had seen die? He hadn't even seen the boy go, and it had probably been quick anyhow, almost painless, not a bad way to go . . .

He walked blindly away from the campsite, in nearly total blackness, paralleling the shore. The unexpected grief broke out more strongly, and he shook all over. He did not know what he was crying over. It was all mixed up: the boy, the Buttermilk, the way people treated you and how you had to kill them, the woman rocking, his fatigue, all of it.

He was so tired and it all hurt so much.

He walked on a little distance, beginning to lose his temper at his own weakness, trying to get everything back under control. Only women cried, right? Only women and babies. Not a man.

But it was such a terrible way to die, the way the boy

had died. It was the stuff of Shed's deepest terror. Water, cold, muddy, all around you, closing you in, getting in your eyes and nose and mouth, and you fought it, but you couldn't win and you had to breathe and you screamed and tried to suck in precious air, but there was only the icy, gagging, killing damned water, and your lungs—your heart—

He stopped suddenly, some difference in his footing warning him.

He forgot the grief and fear in an instant, and gently moved his booted foot.

He had stepped into something that was not characteristic of the gravel all along the shore. This was something cushiony underfoot, with brittle pieces of something in it. Some of the little pieces had snapped under his weight.

With something like a sense of relief, he knelt quickly to see what it was he had found. He felt in the dark and his hands plunged into the fluffy, powdery feeling that could only be campfire ashes.

He felt around in a circle, very carefully. He had his eyes closed against the dark so he could feel better, imagine it visually.

There had been a campfire here on the river bank. A depression in the gravel and mud had been scooped out, and wet driftwood piled in. The fire had burned for several hours, judging by the amount of ash.

It was a very recent campfire. The rain had not made the ash crusty, had not washed much of it out of the depression. There was not even very much rain water in the shallow cavity.

Shed drew his conclusions.

Someone had been along here, and had camped for the night, very recently. His guess was only last night.

Someone who had camped this close to the river must have been *on* the river, just as he was. There was no other reason to climb down through all the rocks, because fresh water was everywhere in the rain and thaw.

So another man—or men—had come down the Buttermilk a day ahead of him. This was very hard to believe, because only someone in a desperate hurry would use the Buttermilk during this flood. Shed had imagined he and his family were alone on its entire length.

But this was not so. Others were ahead of him. Judging by the size of the campfire site, it was a party of at least three men; a lone man, or even a pair, would not have built this big, because finding the wood that might burn was too hard a task.

Standing, Shed turned to look back across the wet, glistening black shoreline to the intensely smoky yellow flare of his own little fire. He let the import of this old fire, here, sink in.

As he did so, he felt a distinct chill.

From the first—from that day when he knew he must leave the cave early this year—there had been the sensation of someone in pursuit. It had ebbed at times, then grown so strong that it was almost a physical force within him. Right now, the short hairs on his neck bristled and he had the knife-like feeling of *another presence nearby*—not so close as to watch, but close by any other standard.

Had he, he wondered, been looking in the wrong direction for whatever it was that was chasing him?

Was the pursuit now *ahead* of him on the river, and,

instead of fleeing from it, was he going somehow to meet it?

It was a very bad feeling. It was very deep. Shed knew enough to recognize that it could not be analyzed or put into words. But it was there, and, being much like an animal, he understood it clearly with a part of himself that did not need words and would have scorned them.

A creature like the panther or the deer died when it gave up hope. But there were other strange deaths. Animals sometimes *knew when they were going to die.* It might be only an instant beforehand, or at least this was as much knowledge as Shed had ever himself witnessed in the startled eyes of a doe, instants before he squeezed the trigger and sent a big slug crashing into its heart cavity. But that did not mean other animals might not, sometimes, know farther in advance, and better.

It was said some fish went upstream to spawn and then to die, and knew why they were going before they even started, and did so reluctantly at first, until the spawning made them forget the rest of their knowledge of the future. Some said coyotes had been known to return to their puppy caves just before the end, although no man could see how the animal knew the time for dying was at hand. Shed could remember a story back in school about elephants doing this, too—going to a hidden place to die alone, and there the earth was littered with their huge bones and great ivory tusks.

He shivered again.

Was he like these? Was his feeling not so much one of pursuit, but of his own nearing death?

He thought about it. He did not want to die. The thought of dying terrified him. He tried never to think about it. To die, and have an end to it, to *rot.* Ah, God. He was afraid of dying.

He walked back toward the campfire. He tried to convince himself he was only very tired. But Jason was gone —*dead.* This other campfire was real. Men were ahead of him on the Buttermilk. He did not understand.

Faith was by the fire as before, rocking.

Shed squatted in front of her. He poked a stick at the fire, making fresh plumes of wet smoke billow out of the yellow flames.

"Buttermilk can't git any worse," he said cheerfully. "I've learned a lot about it, too. You can listen for the roar—tell the worst places. And that old boat. You notice how it starts to shake when it feels bad water coming up on us? You can feel it shake. Like it was afraid, almost. But that helps us: tells us when to be extra-careful.

"The old boat tries to trick you. It'll turn on you if you let it. Only, I don't let it. Not now. I've learned. You catch it early and bring it back around. Then it tries to go the other way, but you stop that, too. Then it goes straight a while. It's a mean boat, but it's strong. Real strong. I've fixed it up again good and it don't hardly leak at all.

"I've figured out how to swing wide on curves, too, to miss snags. Rolling places mean big rocks, so you go around 'em. You can't pole in this current, you got to oar. But I've learned how.

"I've learned plenty," he told Faith. "We'll make it."

Faith did not look at him or show any sign she heard. She rocked endlessly on her hips . . . on those hips he had mounted . . . hips that had given birth.

She was not mad, Shed told himself, studying her. She

would be all right. They would get through. They would beat this old Buttermilk finally, and get through. The river had beaten him once, and had gotten one of his family. But no more.

No more, he thought, squatting by the fire.

EIGHT

In the morning, the weather was better and the river was higher. Shed awoke with a great startled chill, having dreamed about worse losses. He sat up in the wet rocks and took stock.

The sun was just coming up, trying to get through swollen gray clouds. There was a cold mist in the air. To the west, beyond a rocky escarpment, a hole in the clouds allowed a golden shaft of light to come all the way to the ground, where it gleamed on a high, spindly granite platform that rose above its fellows like the tallest monument in a graveyard.

Shed's clothes were still wet. He hurt everywhere. The pain was probably what had awakened him. He had not, however, started so violently that he had awakened anyone else. Faith lay under a canvas across from Shed's position by the dead campfire, and she had the bundled figure of the little girl in her arms. The nearby little blanket mound was Richard, also unstirring.

The boat remained where Shed had beached it, a great, ungainly craft out of the water, rocking slightly with the current.

Shed decided the river was only a little higher.

He got up stiffly and quietly and gathered some twigs, got a tiny fire going. The sounds he made, or the fire's acrid smoke, awakened Faith. She sat up, looked around, found him with her eyes. Shed inwardly cringed, fearing the blank stare of madness. But her eyes were not like that.

He felt an enormous gladness. "You're better," he said.

She looked at him sharply, as if trying to see behind his words. But then, quickly, she seemed to relax. Her lips set in a line.

"Yes," she said.

Shed limped over to the bundled form of the little girl on the ground. She was dead, he thought. But she was not dead. Her color was a sickly yellow now, and her lips were cracked and puffy, and her breath rasped like a file on glass. Her eyes did not open when he touched her. Fire.

Richard still slept.

"We get there tonight, maybe," Shed told Faith.

She said nothing, chewing at a strip of dried meat.

"Can't be worse," Shed added encouragingly. "We get there tonight."

Still she did not respond, so he went on: "Little girl might be all right yet. Richard is good. Richard is fine. You can be fine again. Doctor in Eagle Grove."

Although he watched her carefully, he could see no sign that she heard. Had he been wrong? Was she still crazy? Worried and wanting her to feel good, he walked around the fire and stood beside her, where she ate like a machine.

"I'll do better today," he told her. "Old Buttermilk can't have any worse planned for us today. I'm taking care of you. You'll be fine. Don't feel bad."

And he reached out to awkwardly pat her shoulder.

She hurled his hand back with a vicious movement that startled him. "Oh, *God!*" she gasped. She threw the piece of dried meat at him. It hit him just below the eye, stinging, and dropped to the ground. He staggered back a step.

"What?" he grunted.

"Don't *pat* at me!" she hissed, crouching, her eyes ablaze with loathing.

"What?" he said again, unable to comprehend.

"Don't touch me! Don't fondle at me and try to act like something you aren't! My husband is dead and my son is dead and my daughter is dying. Then all I'll have left is my poor little feeble-minded child, and he'll die, too. We're *all* going to die. I'm not stupid. I know that. Don't kiss at me and pet at me and lie to me!"

She spat the key words, and then, as if exhausted by the outburst, sank to her knees in the wet sand, covered her face with her hands, and began silently to weep.

Shed watched her shoulders tremble with the weeping.

He tried to understand what she had said and what it meant.

Numbed, he turned and walked to the boat. He looked back at the camp. She was still crying, and Richard had sat up and was watching her. Shed felt a great pang for the boy, and then for her, and then for himself.

The attack had been so unexpected he had no equipment for handling it. Her words had hit deep into him, and they hurt. The hurt grew as he tried to comprehend precisely what she had said and what the words meant.

Then, suddenly, the pain changed character and he knew he was going to have a spell.

It swelled out of his chest and gut and burst into his

skull, with a great deal of hot pain this time, as it sometimes happened. Then he saw the boat and sky and water and everything going dim—graying out—and he struggled feebly, and it took him under.

Then, terrified and gagging, he was in the water. He was under the water. He got use of his limbs again and fought, trying to swim, to kick free of the icy wetness engulfing him. He saw brownish light above and he fought for it, his body collapsing inside in pain, and then he burst up into the brightness, turning over and almost instantly going under again.

The instant had been enough. He was in the river, in the current, being carried along, and he had caught part of a breath that sent fiery life through him. He managed to break the top again and remain there, paddling wildly, waves breaking over his head, his nose and mouth full of water with grit in it. He was coughing. He shook his head and tried to see what was going on.

He had had a spell, that was clear enough. And he had fallen forward into the Buttermilk. The current had caught him at once, tumbling him toward the center of the stream. That was where he was now, being borne along swiftly, the icy water sucking at his body. Camp was already behind somewhere. He did not recognize anything. He was disoriented not only by the speed and shock of the rushing water, but by the usual aftermath of a big spell: his skull felt as if it were splitting, and he was going to be sick at his stomach.

He took a few strokes, trying to battle the current to get near shore, and his stomach gave up its thin, bitter contents. He strangled on the vomit and almost went completely under again.

The water, stabbing cold into his vitals, spun him around as he swam. He was in the middle, being carried along very fast. He saw debris in the water with him. Sand in his eyes made things blurry. There was sheer rock on one side and crumbled cliffs on the other. His only chance was to get to the side where spray erupted from the rocks.

After a dozen strokes, he knew the shore was not going to be easy to reach. He could not tell he was making any progress from the center. The water had a thick power to it, rushing so swiftly that it seemed to resist his efforts to go against the grain. Waves splashed over him, making him splutter and gasp. He retched again, doubled up by the pain, opening his eyes under water and seeing an explosion of bubbles and brown froth and dark and light. Then he righted himself again and got his head out of the water long enough for a choking breath.

It was going to kill him now, he thought. He had a sense of great regret. You died when it was your turn; he had learned this in the mountains, seeing so much death through the years. But he had not ever dreamed that he would die this way.

The thought of dying this way, helpless in the damned Buttermilk, made him struggle harder.

Nothing seemed to help. He was gripped by the current and swept along, first with his head out of the water, then being doused again. He tried to swim shoreward, but couldn't make headway. He was being carried on and on, helpless.

What was amazing was how well he kept on top. Every

time he was thrown sideways, or upside down, he went under. But while a part of his mind said he was finished, he should give up, it was not the part that took charge when the cold water pressed against his vision. Then the other part of him took over, the part that was not ready, or willing, to die. Not now, not any time.

He remembered a conversation he had had with a man when he was very little. He had always assumed the man had been some kind of preacher.

"Have you been saved, boy?" the man had demanded fiercely.

Shed had not understood the term.

"Don't you know you are going to *die?*" the man had barked.

"I want to live forever," Shed had told him, baffled.

"No one lives forever! Not in this world! You are going to die!"

"I am!" Shed had told him. "I'm going to live and live and *live!*"

But that had been long ago, and now the damned river had him.

He kept fighting, getting tireder all the time, unwilling or unable to give up. He had to save himself—get back to the others.

The river swept him around a bend, turned him over, and threw him into something big and hard and prickly. He gasped and hung on to something.

He had been thrown into the branches of a big tree snagged up. The water broke over him as he clung trying to get impressions sorted out. He was still out in the stream, but the far end of the tree was lodged in fallen rocks on shore. If he could get through the tree, hanging on—

He went hand over hand. Flesh tore away from his fingers as the river seemed to work harder to get him back. But he kept going. Finally he grabbed a rocky knob and pulled himself ashore. He managed to climb out onto a little rock shelf.

He collapsed. He could feel the force of the river in the rock itself, shaking it from within. He had seen enough rockfalls to know that he could not stay where he was, even for a minute; the shelf was giving way under his weight.

Getting groggily to his hands and knees, he crawled along the shelf. He got to a place where the shelf had already collapsed, making a ditch that led back from the water toward firmer ground. He rolled into the ditch and tumbled down. He fell out onto solid earth patched here and there with muddy weeds. He lay flat, gasping for air.

He was not really hurt. His side was afire, but that was yesterday's injury. His hand felt numb now, although he had used it to fight to get out. Nothing else seemed injured. His heart was in tumult, and he lay still, gasping for more air and listening to his heart.

In a few minutes he began to get things back into focus. He remembered the others and what he had to do.

The only way was to climb. He had to go over the rock walls and follow the river upstream. Otherwise he would be lost and never find the exact spot where he had fallen.

He started.

The rain had gone away and breaks had appeared between the gray clouds, and the sun beat with thin warmth on his body as he climbed. The roar of the Buttermilk pounded all around him. He climbed methodically and well, taking no chances. It was not a dangerous climb for him, only a hard one, and at the top of the formation he looked down the far side and saw, below, the place where they had camped. He saw Faith and the children and the boat.

He went down to them.

Faith's eyes were large and frightened. "I thought you had—you were—"

"No," Shed said.

Her hand raised. She almost reached out to him. But then she let her hand fall.

Shed watched her, puzzled. He had not forgotten the things she had said before his spell, but because he could not understand them he had placed them aside, to consider later. She was not herself, he thought. It was the damned river. Once he got her to town, things would be better.

"We'll go on now," he told her.

She nodded, obedient, and he prepared the boat.

As if driven by whim, the Buttermilk played no new tricks on them for several hours. Shed knew that he might ordinarily have been terrified by the speed of the water, its twisting pools and hidden boulders here and there, but after the first day's journey it seemed less difficult. He kept Faith, with Elizabeth on her back, in the middle of the boat through the morning. Richard he put at the front, a rope around his waist tied to the seat. The boat continuously leaked water from a dozen damaged spots, forcing them to bail with two tin cans. But water did not hurl itself over the side, and in the vees of the canyons ahead the sky was bright blue, filled with sunlight. When the boat did reach one bad place late in the morning, Shed guided it down through a chaos of hidden rocks and exploding spray wih the expert care of a born sailor or river man.

After a while, the Buttermilk smoothed again, the boat gliding through a long, almost placid stretch where the walls on either side showed wet stains a foot higher than the present water level. The river was receding.

It was all going better now, Shed thought. Sometime later in the afternoon he would begin spotting familiar landmarks. There were waterfalls ahead, but he knew where they were. There were more rapids, too, but he could beat them as well. He felt confident.

"Eagle Grove by nightfall!"

"Are we that close?"

"Got to be!"

"How much longer in the boat?"

"Couple hours—four or five, maybe. Not long!"

"Will we stop to rest soon?"

"After bit! Got to keep going right now. Good stretch. We can rest after a bad place, if they are any more."

"Are you all right?"

"*Me?*"

"You look so pale—so worn out."

"Never felt better! Takes more'n a little river to get a mountain man!"

"Your arm—"

"Awyep, it's hurt. But it'll be fine. I'm feeling good—stronger. Takes more'n a little hurt arm to git down an old fool like me. We'll git you there, never you worry about that. You got no cause for worry now. —You see them tall rocks yonder?"

"Yes . . ."

"Chimney Rocks. That's their name."

"You know them?"

"Walked 'em. They tell me it ain't that far yet to Eagle Grove."

"The river is still bad."

"Can't hurt us now. We got things going right along. Awyep. Going right along!"

He decided he would take them as far as the road to Eagle Grove. It would be only a mile or two from there into the town. Faith would only have to follow the road.

Shed knew he badly needed both rest and outfitting. But Eagle Grove was far too dangerous. He would leave the boat and head directly north. Put as much land between him and the law as he could. Straight north, through the western traces of the canyon country, striking out toward the mountains beyond. Within two days, pushing hard, he could be swallowed up again.

The rest of it would be up to her. The traders' post out of Grand Junction was almost always safe. He would tell her about that. If she wanted to study on it and come join him later, that would be the place. By summer's end, they could all be so far northwest that no one would ever have heard of him.

He hoped she would want to do that: join him. Once she was away from the Buttermilk, and thinking back on the things he had done for her and the tykes, she would come to him. Of course she had said bad things this morning, but she was frightened now, and grieving. Once away from this damned river, and rested, she would feel different. He had never wanted a woman or tykes for his own before, but now he did and he felt certain he was going to have them.

It surprised him, in a way, that the clearing weather had so cheered him. Last night, after finding that other campfire's remains, he had been very frightened and low. Now, the work of the river beginning to turn his insides to sludge once more, he was infinitely more cheerful. He told himself he had been borrowing trouble, worrying about others on the river. It had been the dark; that was what had depressed him. The dark had always bothered him, because it made the way he saw things sometimes—*inside* things as well as things that were really out there—more obvious.

He had been very sure last night that he was going down the Buttermilk to his death. The name of the boat seemed to verify this, and Jason's accident was only a first step in a series of Bad Things. At least it had seemed so in the dark: Shed knew that bad things, once they started, came in series and usually climaxed in truly Bad Things, those involving pain and stupidity and meaningless death.

Now, he was not so sure. Scanning the sky, he saw that it continued to clear. His clothing, from the waist up, was fairly dry due to the constant cold wind of moving downstream. He hurt, but he could endure a great deal more. So he permitted himself to imagine the future again.

The endless canyon country went on. More time passed, blurring. They came to a very bad spot where the river was wide but all the water boiled over barely hidden boulders and snags. Shed got the boat close to shore; he gave Faith her instructions about the oar; he went over the side into water so cold and fast that it sucked his breath away; he found footing on slippery hidden rocks with the current tugging and sucking at the level of his chest; he held onto the back of the boat and eased it between boulders, slipping once and hanging on as it almost got away from him, dragging him, but then regaining an angry foothold; he backed *Death* between two great boulders, eased it over a sizzling-fast bed of smaller rocks, managed to control it over a foot-high drop and through an area bordered by a sluggishly turning whirlpool that pulled, with fingers like snakes, at his body, trying to draw him off balance so the boat could be drawn toward the vortex; then he was dragged as the boat went through a deeper fast place where his feet would not touch bottom, and then Faith swung the boat nearer shore and his feet touched again and he got control and they were past the bad place and he climbed back over the high side and tumbled exhausted to the floor of the craft.

Faith, without instructions from him, turned the boat and guided it manfully into deeper current that ran swift and true and smooth. He caught his breath and clambered to her seat and took the oar from her and went to the back again.

They had come into a slightly different area, one where the river twisted between lower spires and minarets and crazy stovepipe formations, with taller buttes and collapsed columns marching off on all sides to jagged horizons. There were only the boat and the river and the rocks, not even any birds. Shed wondered momentarily if there could be anyone else left on earth, and thought how nice it would be if that were the truth, and he could take his family anywhere, and there would be no one trying to kill him or take what belonged to him. But that was too good to be true.

"You done good when I was wore out back there," he told Faith.

She watched him with eyes that glazed from fatigue and grief. "Did I do right?"

"Awyep. I said so, didn't I?"

She stared at the rock formations bordering the river, but her eyes were unseeing.

Shed tried to cheer her. "Old Buttermilk can't fool us now, right? River has a lot of tricks, but we've learned 'em. We worked good on that stretch. Both of us. Did you see me going along there once with my head under? I tell you, I know how an anchor feels. You fall down a slope or something like that, you feel about the same, but you know it's gonna *end*. Slope can't go to China. But I think this old river thought she had me for keeps another time; she wanted to drag me all the way down. Only you had the oar and helped me beat. We done it together."

"Can we stop . . . for a little while . . . soon?"

He pondered this. "Don't see a good place along here. Oughtta find a good place soon."

"I don't want to waste time."

"Awyep. But we gotta stop for a while. We all need to walk a mite."

She stared sightlessly again.

"I had a raft once in Hannibal," Shed told her. "We'd git on my raft and this boy name of Kleitzer, he had a bigger one. We had us wars. Come around a bend, through some brush—bang! there's that other raft, Kleitzer throwing rocks. Git out at night, pole along the crick, couldn't see nothing, sneak up on him; jump onto the end of his raft, tip it over."

Shed laughed aloud, remembering. It had been long since he had remembered this. And then he remembered why he did not think about this set of memories much, because of the way they always ended. A great, angry sadness swept through him.

"I didn't have a maw then," he said. "Kleitzer's folks made him stop. 'Don't play with the crazy boy.' He tole me his own self. But he done it. He quit. I went and waited a lot of times. He never came. I took his raft and tore it up. He told. I got beat."

Faith watched him, but he could not tell what she was thinking.

"I didn't care," he told her.

It was early afternoon when he finally found a good place to stop, a rocky outcropping in a curved sweep of the Buttermilk. Although the current was fast, he beached the boat expertly. He helped Faith climb out with Elizabeth still strapped to her back. Then he helped Richard. By the time he had made sure *Death* was high on the rocks, secure from the deep, fast current that made it tremble, Faith had unstrapped the little girl and was examining her. Shed was amazed. Elizabeth was better, her eyes clearer, her fever definitely down.

"Yes, my baby," Faith whispered to the little girl. "Yes, my baby girl."

Shed took Richard along the steep slope to some brush, and there relieved himself. Richard, seeing the action, also unbuttoned his trousers and made a stream of yellow water that danced on the green weeds.

"That's better, eh?" Shed asked him. "I was about to bust!"

Richard paid attention to his business.

"Take good care of that thing," Shed advised him, man to man. "Know'd lots of men that lost a finger or even a hand, they could git along just fine. But there's things you want to watch after, right? A man's just got one of them there things to last all his life, right? That's right. You understand every word I'm saying, you little bugger. Sure."

Richard finished and watched Shed, who was still going.

"One of these days," Shed told him, "you'll find out other things that thing is good for. Oh, yeah. You sure will. But that's down the road a piece, huh? Sure it is.

"We'll go on back to your momma and your little sister and see if we can't finish off the last of that dried meat. Sound good to you? Sure it does!

"Listen, boy. Dried meat has got more men through bad things than any other food. You recollect that when you get older. You make a kill, you salt and dry some, right? And you wrap it, right? All right, then.

"By nightfall, way I figure it, you'll be having better food. But we'll just eat this up anyways. We got that one falls to get past yet. Won't be easy. But this God-damned river has had her last say, far as I'm concerned. You agree? Sure you do! We'll eat, rest a while, get going. Eagle Grove inside five, six hours! How's that sound to you, huh?"

They went back to the campsite. Faith had started collecting sticks for a fire, against the cool wind. Shed helped, and soon had a good blaze going. The smoke coming off the flames worried him a little, but he knew the country and assumed it was all right. He got out the dried meat and they ate of it. He was heartened when even Elizabeth tried weakly to chew on a strand of it. Then Elizabeth seemed to fall asleep again, and Richard sat beside one edge of the fire and played with some round pebbles, and he got out the pipe and sucked on it, wishing for tobacco.

"How long?" Faith asked him.

"Few hours, I think."

"The river was better today."

"Worst is over."

"I . . . said some things this morning that I shouldn't."

"Don't matter."

"No, but I—"

"You had cause."

"But I know how much you're doing for us. You're doing everything you can. You didn't have to try to help us."

Shed sucked the pipe and watched her. She had thinned magically, and there were black hollows beneath her eyes. Her clothing and her stringy hair were wet, matted with sand. He felt a deep, insistent pulse of desire for her. But that wouldn't be good for Richard to see, he thought, so he put it away.

Faith seemed driven to say something more. "Something . . . happened to you this morning."

"Foot slipped," Shed lied.

"And when you fell down that slope."

"I'm clumsy, that's all."

"You . . . fainted."

"No."

"You're sick."

"No!"

"What is it, then? What happened?"

"Nothing happened! I slipped! People slip. People fall. I paid no mind to where I was going—slipped. Ain't nothing wrong with me! Now leave it alone!"

She lowered her face. "I'm sorry."

Face burning, Shed climbed to his feet. Pain lanced him. "Nothing to be sorry about. Now c'mon. We got to git."

She nodded, stood, and picked up Elizabeth. Stiffly he helped her fit the little girl into the straps on her back, tightening them. He kicked dirt over the fire, gathered up the few items they had left, tied them in the cloth bag, and carried them to the boat. Faith and Richard stood watching while he wrestled the boat off the gravel embankment. The deep, fast current, even though the river was very wide here, tugged at the boat, making it unstable.

Still angry with her, Shed held the boat by main force with its nose on the rocks. He gestured with his head and she stepped forward, moving clumsily with the child on her back, to climb into the boat.

She leaned out with one hand on the side rail and put her leg inside. As she did so, the current made the boat bob up and down, and swing a little from shore. She was thrown off balance.

Seeing what was happening, Shed yelled hoarsely and hauled with all his might to get the boat farther up on the shore.

But it was too late. The boat was swinging out—in a wide, lazy arc—and it pulled Faith off the steep bank. She teetered for an instant, awkward under the bundle on her back, and then plunged into the water with a huge splash.

Shed screamed and lunged for her. The boat swung back, going right over the spot where she had hit. He looked on the far side for her and saw nothing.

"Faith!"

He plunged into the water after her, although he could see nothing. The icy impact took him under the boat, sucking the air out of his shocked lungs, and he felt the current twist like a beast, sucking at him, and if he hadn't banged into the rock wall of the bank—it went straight down—he would have been carried away instantly.

He came up spluttering and sobbing and saw nothing in the water—no one—just Richard, standing at the very brink, looking down at him.

"Get back from there! Get back!"

Shed heaved himself out of the water, grabbed Richard, and carried him back to the place the fire had been. Sitting him down roughly, he ordered him to stay there. Then he turned and ran back to the bank.

The current had pressed the boat against the shore, where it clung. The river lurched along, twisting, broad here, the color of blood in the sunlight, its oily surface gleaming.

Shed looked up and down.

"Oh Jesus Christ," he moaned. "Oh Jesus Christ. Oh Jesus Christ."

NINE

Shed could not believe it. He simply could not believe it.

There had to be a mistake.

He turned and ran to his right, along the steep bank, scrambling over a rock pile, tumbling down the far side, running again on mud. The river curved, and he ran along a low shelf that jutted into the water, his eyes searching. He could not see a sign of the woman or the child she had carried on her back. The river tumbled along with deep, swift currents, roiling here and there, broad, brown-red. The far shore was composed of vertical rock cliffs that rose hundreds of feet. Shed's present position on the outcropping allowed him to look well downstream, to a point where the channel narrowed sharply and the water seemed to run even faster. He couldn't see anything. There was no sign of anyone in the water.

He ran back the way he had come, still watching the river. Going over the rockfall near the campsite, he fell again and hurt his aching bad arm. He ran past the killed fire—Richard sitting there, watching vacantly—and went on around the other side of the outcropping so he could get a view upstream. It was crazy to look upstream and he knew it, but he did it anyway.

Going back to the campsite out of breath, he looked at Richard and at the buried fire and at the boat. He looked out at the river again, scanning. He went to the bank and stared at the spot where she had fallen. Then he thought she might be under the boat, somehow, and he wrestled it along the shore a few yards, almost losing it once. But the water where the boat had been was like all the rest of the river, empty.

He stood there wringing his hands.

He could not believe it, because things just did not happen that quickly, or without warning. There was always a warning in nature for everything, even a rock-slide. You only had to read the signs. But here there had been nothing and it made no sense.

People did not just vanish that way when they fell into water, even ice-cold water in flood like this. They came up. They struggled. Sometimes they yelled and came up several times. Even if the current took you away, you came up. Shed had come up when he fell. She should have come up too. People didn't just vanish. . . . The river could not have won again this easily—casually.

He turned to the remaining little boy. "You know what happened, boy? I'll tell you. She slipped and went in. You think she drowned? No. I don't think so. You don't drown that way, quick. You think she went under and that's it, but she didn't. She couldn't have.

"I think she got carried downstream too fast. That's what happened to me, you remember? Awyep. It takes you fast. It took her fast. She went, and it took her. But she's strong, she'd fight. She wouldn't just go under. The river couldn't beat her easy.

"She went in and got took down a ways. Probably right now she's on down there, climbing out. Just like I did. She'll need some help, boy. And a fire. We'll build her a good fire, right? Dry her off. Make her feel better. Only, we'd better hurry."

Carrying Richard to the boat, Shed put him on the floor near the center seat. He looped the rope, tied to the seat, around the boy's middle and tied it fast. Then he shoved the boat off and began oaring hard, one side and then the other, hurling the boat along in the current.

They went around the bend and hurried along toward the narrower place, Shed watching the water and the banks carefully. "See her in a minute, boy! You watch too, you hear? Good! You watch! She'll be glad to see us, you can count on that! Scary, gettin' thrown in that way, carried along."

He was so sure he was right, he felt considerably better for a little while. He kept grinning at Richard to keep his spirits up, and it worked for him, too, keeping his own up. Any minute now, he thought, he would see a movement along the banks somewhere.

The boat hurtled down through some light rapids and into a long gorge, very narrow, where the walls came down to the water's surface at right angles. It was far from the campsite now, but Shed told himself she could not, after all, have climbed out along here. She had to have gone farther.

The river bent again, its roar slackening slightly, and there were sandy, debris-littered banks on both sides again, the stone walls and turrets back a little from the bed. He scanned the banks, talking a blue streak. But he saw no one.

Digging the oar deep on one side only, he guided the boat out of the mainstream and in to the shore on the left. As the front scraped sand and mud, he hopped out and pulled the boat aground again. He untied Richard, set him ashore, showed him where to sit on a rock back from the water, pulled the boat up a little, cupped his hands over his eyes to scan again.

There was no one and nothing and it was too far. He had come too far now. No one could have made it this far.

He sat down heavily in the mud, splashing, as the realization finally hit with full force.

There was just no way to pretend. It was like one of the bad dreams, but it was no bad dream, he was awake. He had lost her. Her and the little girl both. Gone. The river had won again.

It was hard to believe, because Shed had seldom really tried for something and failed to win it. He had learned early not to ask for much, but to fight for what he really had to have. When he truly had to have something, he had always managed to win.

Now he had not won at all. He knew he had done many bad things, and was not really a very good person. But you had to be this way to survive. And bringing the family down the Buttermilk—that was a *good* thing, a right thing to do, one of the few right things he had ever tried to do in his entire life. It seemed wrong to lose when you were doing a right thing.

And he had wanted her so much. It had seemed so proper, figuring out how he would leave her and where they would meet again. She might have delayed, but in the end she would have obeyed him. There was a God somewhere. He did not amount to much and just sat around smoking his pipe most of the time, but He was not actually a bad God, only an indifferent one. It was not fitting for even an indifferent God to have something like this happen.

Shed sat in the mud, breathing hard, and stared out at the river.

Watching the river and thinking of nothing, Shed began to hate the river. He had never liked it, and had feared it. But now, slowly, a different feeling grew. He recognized the feeling as hate, and studied it carefully.

It was, after all, the river's fault. The God-damned Buttermilk.

Not that the river could think like a man. But the river was a real thing. It had a character. It swelled up and burst through things and tore them away, and tried to kill people, and just kept moving, uncaring, killing what it could.

"You God-damned Buttermilk," Shed said softly, watching it. "You took the one tyke but it wasn't enough. You had to take her and the girl both. You want everything. A man might look at you and say you were just a river, but you ain't just a river, you God-damned bastard, I hate you.

"You can't just have everything, you son of a bitch," he told the river. "You think you can beat me, but you had me and I beat *you*. You grab you the people you can, like the woman and the tykes. But I'm still here. You can't get me."

Then, remembering suddenly about Richard, he turned. Richard was playing with mud a few paces away, intent on his gooey task.

Shed looked back at the river. "Nor him.

"You can't get him, neither, Buttermilk. Haven't you

got enough? Do you think you're getting more? You ain't getting no more and I mean it!"

The river coursed along, pretending to ignore him.

He turned and watched Richard play in the mud. The little boy was making mud pies and piling them one atop the other. He had a stack of seven or eight, and, as Shed watched, the pile tipped over. Richard solemnly began making pies for a new stack, as if nothing had happened.

Somewhere, searching along the banks or coming downstream, Shed had hurt his arm much worse. He knew it was broken now. There was a lump just below the elbow and he thought it was the bone, and it throbbed with a fiery, insistent pain. But he did not give it much attention. As he watched Richard play, he felt something much sharper and deeper, such a pulse of love that he thought he was going to have a spell again.

It was not right for Richard, either, he thought: any of it. The tyke deserved a home and a mother and a father, not a place on the bank of this God-damned evil river, with a crazy man who had never been any 'count.

Or maybe, Shed thought suddenly, God had planned it this way.

Richard was, after all, like him. They both had something wrong with their heads. And as long as Richard was alive, and he was alive, they had each other, and maybe that was how it was supposed to be.

It was not like it was all over, Shed thought. He would take Richard to Eagle Grove. That would beat the river and seal the compact, because he would still have done what he set out to do, get them there if he could. He had not lost everything. Richard was young and had a long life ahead of him, and Shed could help him live it. Shed could teach him everything.

He thought about this, and clouds scudded across the sky, making it dull gray.

A large raindrop splattered on his forehead, awakening him from the daze or spell he had been under.

He got to his feet, decided.

He walked over to Richard. "Hey, boy, making pies? Awyep. Recollect when I did that. Only don't try to eat 'em. I tried to eat one oncet. Taste like tarnation, I'll tell you that."

The boy looked up at him, blank.

"We're going on down," Shed told him, picking him up and holding him in his arms so he could talk eye to eye. "Now I know how you feel about your momma. I feel bad too. A man's got to learn to take his sadness. A man can take just about anything. You remember that. You think you can't, but then it comes and you can take it no matter what.

"So we're going right on down. You and me. Right? And you don't worry none. I got you. Nothing is going to happen to you. I'm taking good care of you, and when John Riley Shed gives his word, it's as good as gold.

"Your momma was . . . your momma was a good woman, boy. The best. She was the best I ever saw. You're going to miss her a whole lot. You won't never stop missing her, there's no sense me trying to lie to you about that. Funny thing . . . I never even knew my momma, but I think about her. I even dream about her . . . think what she must have looked like, how it would've felt for somebody to hold you . . . love you . . ."

Shed shook himself and looked more directly into Richard's eyes. "No sense telling you you'll forget. You won't. I won't, neither. You'll go along . . . miss her." Shed was having trouble with his eyes: they were watering or something. "But you got to keep going, you savvy?

"Life ain't easy for nobody, Richard. Never has been. The Good Book says man has got to earn his keep by the sweat of his brow. It don't say in there nowhere you'll have a life of milk and honey. There ain't no milk and honey. People will try to git you any way they can. People are . . . people. Sometimes, if you're off alone someplace, you can git to thinkin' a lot of people are good, and some are . . . some are. Most ain't. They'll make fun of you. They'll cheat you if they can, steal from you if they can, lie in your face and stick a knife in your back.

"That's just the way people are.

"But that don't mean you ought to quit, you understand me? Your momma was . . . good. God-damned Buttermilk!"

Shed walked with Richard toward the boat.

"Don't need to think life's over, because it ain't. No, sir. Not for you, not for me. We ain't quitting, right? Right. We can be tough, too, right? Right. I ain't leaving you and I ain't giving up on you or nothing else. Now you listen to me. I aim to go right on taking care of you. You're all right. I'm going to tie you in that there boat and there ain't nothing can happen to you, and when we get outta the boat I'm holding you by the hand and nothing can happen and you ain't gonna be skeert. Do you understand me?

"God-damned right you understand me. We understand each other, right? We're alike, right?

"You ready? Good. You need to pee or anything? No?

Good. Come on, now. Here we go. You and me. That's it."

He put Richard into the boat and tied him to the middle seat, leaving a foot or two of slack so the boy could move around a bit in the bottom of the boat, but not go anywhere even if a wave hit him and tried to take him over the side. Richard might get doused, but that was the worst that could happen, with the rope. Shed knew he could grab the rope and have the boy back within seconds. It was a good arrangement and Shed carefully explained it to Richard.

With the boy tied in, he looked up and down the river once more, thinking how fine it would be to find her now—to see movement, or a hand waving, and then the glad reunion. He imagined it so vividly and with such intensity that he wondered why it didn't happen. But there was nothing, no movement, only the rocks and the damned Buttermilk and the sky gathering its clouds again rapidly.

"People all my life try to tell me I ain't worth nothing," Shed told Richard. "Maybe so. But I got you. I ain't worthless. I got *you*. I thought, Well, I can take 'em all down that river. But I was skeert. It tricked me, this Buttermilk. A lot. Only it can't take *everything*. I never owned stuff and I have the spells. But I got what I need. Somebody might say, Well, that old Shed, he warn't worth nothing, he lost his family. But it ain't so. I got you. You understand me? Sure."

Shed pushed the boat off the rocks and clung to it, delaying his jump on board a moment because he had Richard fixed with his eyes, and the point was very important to make.

"I'm taking you to Eagle Grove, boy. Now they're setting down there all nice and warm, playing their cards, saying, That Shed, he won't come in here, we got a church and a town marshal and guns and our card games and all them nicey-nicey choir deals and all the rest, and nobody like that old Shed will come in *here*. Well, let me tell you. I'm taking you there. Any son of a bitch try to stop us, you and me, he'll have his guts in his boots, right? I'm *taking* you there."

Richard stared at him, and slowly put one dirty, chubby finger in the corner of his mouth and sucked it.

Shed shoved the boat off and sprang in at the last instant, trying to catch himself with the broken arm. The pain almost made him pass out, but he tried to hide this from the boy. *Don't fret him none.* He grasped the oar handle with his good hand, awkwardly, steering. The current caught *Death* and swung her out with steely hands, grasping her and taking her along.

Light rain spattered Shed's face as he steered around the bend. Looking beyond, he saw a split in the stream, a kind of shale-strewn island, very narrow and just above water, in the center of the channel. The little island was only shattered rocks and gleaming pink mud, a devastated thing. Shed blinked the cold rain out of his eyes and studied the two streams around the island, figuring which way to go.

Something caught his eye on the edge of the island, on the right side.

He stared, and his flesh prickled with shock. He felt a burst of heat through his bloodstream.

There was something there: a humped-up, rounded shape.

"Oh my God," Shed said. "Listen. Hey. Oh, God!"

The current was carrying the boat swiftly toward the island, and the figure came into clearer view. It might be a sack, Shed told himself, but then he saw it could not be a sack. It might be a dead animal, a deer or something, and there was no use getting your hopes up; when you got your hopes up you were always disappointed. But it was not a dead animal.

It was long and low—the form of a person.

And it stirred.

Shed was screaming at the top of his voice as he oared the boat.

The figure moved again and raised up on arms.

"I see you!" Shed bellowed. *"I see you! It's us! We found you! Here we come! I see you! It's you and we found you!"*

Ignoring the agony that drove into his shoulder and back, he used both hands on the oar as the river tried to sweep *Death* on by. Shed waged the fight automatically, watching the figure on the shore constantly. It was his woman. It was Faith. There she was. She had raised herself up and knelt on the muddy rocks, watching. She was covered with mud herself, a clay figure, her clothing unrecognizable, her face and arms and hair all mud, the same pink-brown of the silt covering the rocky island. But she was alive and she was right there and Shed made the boat swoop into the edge of the island and slam hard into rocks and silt, beaching.

Shed jumped out of the boat and ran to her. He threw himself down and caught her in his arms. He hugged her. He was crying. She was slippery with the mud and like rubber in his arms, like a doll.

But she was real.

"We didn't think you could come down this far," Shed told her. "We stopped. We hunted. We talked it over. We looked good. I thought maybe we could find you but we didn't. I'd give up. I told the tyke we'd make it. I thought you might fall in and go on down and keep up, like I done, and finally come out, but this God-damned Buttermilk, I thought it had you for sure but it didn't, here you are. What happened? Did you git bad hurt? Have you been here a long time? Did you think we'd give up, or got lost our own selfs? I can put you in the boat. We can find a place and build a fire."

He paused and held her back at arms' length and stared at her hard. Her eyes were quite the most terrible thing he had ever seen, and there were twin white rivulets in the mud on her face where the tears streamed. Her lips trembled and she tried to say something, but couldn't.

Shed, his hands moving to her back to draw her close again, encountered the straps of the pack. But then he understood, because the straps were loose, torn.

Elizabeth.

"Where is she?" Shed asked.

Faith stared at him.

Shed shook her so hard her teeth clattered. "Where *is* she? Which way was she going when you seen her last? Along here? Close to here? Could she might of got ashore farther down? How did them straps break? Listen to me. Listen! You've got to *tell* me!"

"Rocks," Faith said hoarsely, her eyes unfocused. "Deep. Felt her go—straps—my little girl—"

"Where? Here? Off this side?"

"Way back up there," Faith said. "Far. Deep . . . so deep and cold for a little girl—I know she's gone. Like Jason. Like—" She broke, and bent forward as if collapsed from within, her head bending over her knees until it rested against the mud.

She wailed.

TEN

So the reality was not at all like the fantasy. Shed had imagined how good it would be to find her again, and cheat the Buttermilk, but now she was alive again but the river had won another battle: she was no longer an entire woman, because too much had been taken from her.

Shed watched her weep, and then looked at the river and the rocks and the sky, and then he wondered if now his situation was not impossible.

He tried to talk to her. He told her how sick Elizabeth had been, and how she might have died anyway. He talked about Richard, who remained, watching with stricken, mute eyes. That seemed to help a little: Faith controlled the weeping, and finally knelt in the mud with her face more composed, under a terrible control.

"We're going on down," Shed told her. "No sense trying to stay here. We can't anyway: no food and no shelter. Well, we might hit out crost country, but it'd be a far piece . . . real far . . . and you and the tyke need rest and that doctor. It ain't all that far now and we can make it. I'm takin' you there, just like you said at your house. Like I said I would."

Faith watched him with terrible eyes, and then nodded.

Shed tried to explain to her that it would have been

necessary, at any rate, to take them on down the river, because the river could not be allowed ultimate victory. But he said this badly and got mixed up in the middle of trying to explain it, which only proved what he had always believed: you didn't say the truly important things; they were simply *known*.

He helped Faith back into *Death*. She took the front seat as before. She seemed almost not to know Richard was there, so Shed tied the boy to the center seat section before shoving off.

The river took them into the deeps of new canyons. A whirlpool tried to take them almost immediately, and Shed got them through it. He was drenched again and his arm hurt much worse. He shivered continually. He felt faint and weak, as if he might have fever. It was difficult to maintain concentration, but he attributed this to fatigue.

The rain came back, teeming down. *Death* went through a long, straight gorge where the rock walls rose straight up hundreds of feet, and then went into a section of canyon where the walls fell back and churchlike spires and chimneys marched off like soldiers. Now and again, Shed got a more distant view as the rain slackened, but all he could see were other ravines, canyons, spiral-shaped formations, tables, cones, buttes, needles, doughnuts of rock, canyons and earthen splits of enormous size and grotesque variety. Only the river was at home in this land, he thought. Only the river belonged. It was a vast, dead land, swollen, glistening, coldly empty during thaw and flood, and a baking, barren hell alive with snakes during other times of the year. Not even the snakes were apparent now, however. Shed and his family were alone.

Time passed and the river seemed to change character. It became, under the steady rain that pocked its sludgy surface, more sullen and gray. Now and then it roiled, vomiting foam from its guts. But mostly it ran almost smooth, heavily, very very fast.

Trying to fool him, Shed thought. Trying to make him think it was not evil. But he would not be fooled.

He knew. The river was an enemy. He had to be on guard against it every moment. He had to outsmart it with cunning. He had been learning all his life how to outsmart things like this river. Nothing else mattered.

"Ain't as bad along here as it was," he told the woman and the boy through chattering teeth. "That don't mean it ain't bad ahead, because it is. But I'm ready for it. Don't you fret.

"I know you think I'm just an ignorant old boy," he told Faith cheerfully. "But lemme tell you something. I been takin' care of myself since I was a tyke not much bigger'n him. Awyep. My paw had his own ideas about how a man should grow up, see? 'Git your schoolin', git your learnin' down, a man's nothing without his learnin'.' That's what he'd say. Then you'd go to school an' old Mister Wheeler, or Mizz Davidson, you'd make a little mistake that didn't count for nothing, and they'd beat on you. Old Mister Wheeler beat on my hands one time till they split here at the joints, see? You can still see the marks. And Mizz Davidson, she'd back you up against the stove, beat on you with a hickory, not care where she hit you, neither. And everybody else laughing.

"Mizz Davidson did it once too often, I'll tell you. I was after school my own self, nobody else, and she started in on me. So what was a man supposed to do? I whacked her. Right. Whacked her good. Run off. Down by the river. Hid. Then at night I heard 'em huntin' me. My own paw went by, close. I heard 'em talkin'."

Shed sighed. "I didn't mean to hurt her, much less kill her. But then they come with the dogs and what's a man to do? Go down-river. Right.

"But once you do a thing, they never let you go any more. Can you imagine a tyke not much bigger'n Richard here, with posters out on him? 'Shoot to kill,' it says?

"I know what you're thinkin'. Go back to your paw, take your medicine. Awyep. Only my paw, he was only there once in a while. He'd left long before. *Long* before. Then when your mother is dead, who's left to stick up for you? So you do what you got to do, right? You make it, right?

"Oh, I'm not saying it was easy. Bunch of men took me on as a cook down around Little Rock. For a while it was okay. Then this one man came to me in the night. I know there ain't things that are fitten to talk about with a woman or a tyke. I ain't going to talk about 'em. But what he tried to do to me . . . what he held me down and done . . ."

Shed shook his head violently to rid himself of the memory. "I took care of *him* later. It wasn't that hard to do. You just wait, let a man get alone, and make sure your knife is sharp.

"What was I supposed to do? Nothing? And let him come back *another* time? And another after *that?*"

He paused, studied the river ahead, scoured rain from his aching eyes with the knuckles of his good, right hand.

"You learn to make your own way," he told his family. "Two or three times, you get laughed at, or beat on, or

. . . something else, you learn. There might be people in this old world that lets theirselfs be a mat for wiping feet on. I ain't one of them. No sir. I lit out after doing for Jasper Corvin—that was his name—and they chased after me a while, and got out more paper, but I taken care to hide good.

"Summer in these mountains, if you got water, you think it ain't so bad. But in the high mountains, comes winter, it can be real bad. Real bad. Iffen you don't know what you're doing, you can die real easy.

"Well, maybe I should of died. But I didn't. Too ornery, huh? Or too smart. People all my life said, 'Shed, you're stupid and ignorant. Shed, you're ignorant and stupid and you have spells.' But a lot of them that said it are dead now, and I ain't. I'm here. I survive. Now, I hear a lot of talk now and again about there being a lot more to it than that, surviving. All about the Good Book and God and all the rest. Maybe so. Maybe so. But I know what *I* got to do. There's only one thing I got, and that's *me,* right? I keep me safe. You maybe think I'm ignorant and stupid, too. But I'm *here,* right? And I'll tell you what. There ain't many men that could have got us this far. Not many could git us down this Buttermilk. And I'm gittin' you right on to Eagle Grove.

"That's right. I'm takin' you. Folks'll know me there, but I might can git in and out fast enough. If not, I can git away. I done before and I can do again. Just like this here Buttermilk; it can't whip me. I'm too ignorant."

He chuckled, but recognized the hollow sound in the chuckle. He was trying to cheer them up somehow. They had to believe in him, he saw, or none of it was any good. So he tried.

But, inwardly, a part of him was as despairing as Faith appeared. In the brief time she had been in the river and away from him, he had allowed the dream to grow about what it might be like to find her again. He had imagined, without fully knowing it, that he would find her and Elizabeth on a safe shore, together. He would recognize her and, whooping and hollering, get to shore and grab her, and she crying and everything, running to him—

"*I was so frightened—*"

"*Awyep, I know—*"

"*We couldn't get out for so long and we thought you were gone—*"

"*We kept comin', tryin' to find you—*"

"*I know you did, I know that now—*"

"*Won't let nothing more happen—*"

"*We need you, John Riley Shed. I didn't know it. I thought you were ignorant. But we can't go on without you, we owe you everything—*"

And she would be crying, clinging, her wet arms around his neck.

And the fantasy had even gone further, he saw now, because he had imagined (since she was dead and anything was possible) how she would go with him somewhere, to the Oregon country maybe, and him in a house, with his pipe, smoking good tobacco and no spells or anything like that, nobody after him or them either, and her fixing supper and the tykes playing on the floor, as he had sensed it had once been in that cabin back there on the slope, before the fever came.

But none of that was going to be, he reminded himself now. He was what he was, and that was a mountain man. You didn't change your spots. And she was half crazy now, maybe would stay that way. Nothing to do but go on with what was left, which wasn't much. Don't hope and you won't be disappointed.

The rain slackened. Shed went on. They came to a narrows where water exploded over hidden rocks and snagged trees. The boat tried to turn broadside, naturally, but Shed caught it and kept it straight. The current got them going so fast everything blurred and was terrifying, but there was a narrow place in the center of the blockage of rocks and trees where the water gushed clean, and Shed made *Death* hit this clear place perfectly, straight on. The craft leaped through and was spat out the far side before anything bad could happen, and then a whirlpool tried to get them again and they went around four or five times, but Shed broke free. They had a brief, mad, scary ride over rocks that cluttered and banged the bottom of the boat, but it was shallow and not really too bad, and then they went past that, too.

Shed thought about the men on the river ahead of him, and wondered who they were and what they wanted. They were good, he thought, because he had seen no signs of boat wreckage. Did they have anything to do with him, and the feeling of pursuit that still prickled along his short hairs?

It was not worth thinking about right now, he told himself.

Hours dragged past.

It was getting late in the afternoon when he saw, up ahead, a great rock formation like a crooked chimney, towering over all the others around it. He had been watching for it. He saw it from far off, then lost sight of it, then swept through a gorge that it towered over like a place of gods, and he saw it close up and knew it was the right one.

He had been at this place before, long ago. He had stood up there on the side of the thing, the sun so hot it shriveled the skin and made the rock too hot to touch, the heat coming up through the soles of his boots, the flies buzzing and the sky a coppery dome, nothing but death on every side. He had looked down at the Buttermilk, like a little ribbon far below, and had hiked down to it to be cooler, and to have water for his jug.

From this place, the falls were not far away.

There were two falls, not especially big ones, but much too high for anyone to make it over them in a boat when the water was up as it was now. There was heavy froth and foam, with big boulders everywhere, and then a downsloping pellmell run, and then a twist in the river's course and the first of the falls, the larger one, about ten feet high, and then a pool that spun, and then the smaller falls, about four feet, and then a maelstrom of white water boiling out into a wider place.

The river was getting out of the most jagged canyons now, and the banks were choked with cedars and firs in the fallen rocks. This gave Shed a much better place to ground the boat than he might have had earlier, and he had counted on this.

He used the white water above the falls to give *Death* momentum enough to break out of the main current and shunt sideways to the brushy, rock-strewn bank. Hopping out, he managed to drag the boat partway onto the shore, and then he climbed back in and untied Richard and carried him out under his arm.

He sat Richard on a log and told him to stay put, but then thought better of it and went back to the boat and got the short length of rope used for tying to the seat, untied it, took it ashore, and fixed it so Richard could not stray, tying one end to the log and the other to the boy's ankle.

Faith clambered out of the boat and watched.

"Do you have to do that?" she asked, surprising him.

"Awyep," Shed grunted.

"I can watch him."

"Good. You watch and leave the rope be. That way we're twice as safe."

She looked at the falls. She could not see the second set from here because of a high rock formation and brush. "How are you going to get around it?"

"Watch," Shed told her.

Going to the boat again, he unlashed a big coil of rope he had brought all the way from Bung's Ferry. He tied one end securely to the iron ring in the front of the boat. It was awkward work with only one hand, but his left arm was useless now, broken. He uncoiled the rope, played the other end out to a small but stout tree near the water's edge, looped it around the tree.

"Nothing to it!" he boasted for the benefit of his family.

Getting two loops of rope around his waist, he went to the boat and carefully pushed it off into the current. It swung out, empty, bobbing more lightly in the water, and the current swung it out and took it down toward the first falls. It reached the end of the rope, as much as Shed had played out, and jolted to a halt, the back end coming around to the front. The tree took the shock on the line, and Shed felt only a quick tightening of the pressure, which the loops around his body bore nicely.

Cursing his useless arm, he played the rope out slowly, backing the boat to the falls. The trembling and battering increased as the boat got closer, and water foamed over its front. It reached the brink of the drop-off and Shed braced himself, but even then, as the boat really tipped and went over, with the slowness of movement in a nightmare, the shock transmitted along the rope jerked Shed to his knees. He managed to hang on. The rope pressure slacked off and the boat righted itself below the falls, twirling around, trying to go around a little bend in the channel and out of sight. Shed played out the last of his rope and let the boat go until it vanished and the rope pressure was very gentle.

"That was the bad one," he told his family. "Other one will be some easier."

He looked at Faith. "You see?"

But she had retreated again into whatever madness was in her. She only stared.

Shed decided he would not try to talk to her. It was too confusing. He would talk to Richard. At least he expected no answer from the boy.

"Understand that, boy?" he asked. "Sure you do! Remember it!"

Snubbing his rope under a boulder, he scrambled through trees and around the bend.

In the foamy pool beneath the falls, the boat turned lazily, half filled with muddy water, straining against the rope that still extended up over the falls and back around the corner to the snubbing place. The pool here was not even deep enough to cover a man's head.

Chuckling, Shed waded into the pool and caught the rope and hauled the boat into shore. He got it aground, untied the rope, and hurried back to the far side.

"Can't fool an old fool," he chortled to Richard as he untied the rope, now slack in the water, and eagerly hauled it back in. "God-damned Buttermilk thinks it can win everything, but we're almost there, now. Another couple hours, that's all. Lower the boat down the other falls, just like this one, and then it's better on down there, except for one bad spot I know about ahead of time. John Riley Shed is taking care of you, boy, you hear me?"

Throwing the coiled rope over his shoulder, he lifted Richard and carried him up the steep rock pile and down the other side, struggling for balance, and to the first pool. He was elated.

The second falls was easier than the first, and he could observe the whole operation as he played out line. He watched the boat back up to the brink, pause as he held tight to the singing rope, then tip high, front in the air, as he let the rope burn around his hips and play out. Somehow, two boards got knocked loose below the smaller falls, and the boat wallowed badly as he dragged it ashore another time. But the nails remained in the sprung planks and he hammered them back in with a rock.

It leaked a little when he got it back into the water, but not too much.

"Everything's all right now, boy!" Shed said, lifting Richard back into the boat and tying him again to the length of rope attached to the middle seat. "Awyep, everything is just *fine!* No more falls. We go on down here an hour, maybe two; then we see the bridge, we walk it in from there. You just set tight, huh? Old John Riley Shed will get you there safe, don't fret none." And he gave Faith his best grin.

In reality, there was at least one more bad place to get through, and he knew it. Somewhere up ahead there was a length where the river tumbled through broken rock, moving swiftly. But he considered how high the water was now, and figured that in this place the flood level would help. The river would simply skim over the rocks and roughness, the high level putting snags and dangers well below the surface. After what he had already been through, he figured this last spot would not be significant.

The truth was that his success at the falls had restored Shed's confidence. His losses ached, a void in his being that would last long . . . long. But you had to go on. You didn't quit or think about bad things that had happened. And the river simply couldn't do any more; he had outsmarted it now.

He kept the boat moving smartly downstream. Here the river was sometimes narrow and very swift, with its current gushing between sheer walls only thirty or forty feet apart. A little later, the river spread out and became almost placid, muddy and viscous-looking, as it crossed terrain of lesser ruggedness, the formations tumbled broken boulders.

Shed knew they were working out of the canyon deeps and soon would be beyond the last predictable bad place. His arm had begun to swell badly, the fingers puffy and purple. His side throbbed. But he kept up a constant chatter at Richard hunkered in the middle of the boat. He had to keep Richard's spirits up. If he could, he had to keep Faith partly sane, too. He was responsible for them, and this responsibility was heavier right now than it had ever been . . . as he felt them drawing nearer Eagle Grove, and other people, and the Danger.

But it felt good, too, to be responsible.

"We might have us some real food again tomorrow this time," he said. "Another hour or two on this old Buttermilk and we're there. It's a far walk from the landing, but we can make 'er. Just one more hour or so on this damned Buttermilk, and then we can camp, dry out.

"We'll walk in," he told Richard and Faith cheerfully. "Get there tomorrow night. Find the doctor, turn you over to him, right? Awyep. I can't stay in town. You know that, don't you? Towns is for ordinary folks. But I tell you what. I ain't just walking off from you. No sir. No ma'am. I can stay around close, you see? I'll make sure you're all right. Have you got other folks someplace? Well, if so, fine. You might need to go to them. No skin off my old nose. But if you ain't, why, that's just fine, too. You could always come with me. Sure you could.

"Oh, I know what you're thinking. Maybe you're right. But what I'm saying is, you ain't got to be alone. If they treat you bad, you ain't all alone. I'll watch. I'll hide. I can do it. Done it before. You don't need to be skeert of nothing. Anybody treat you bad, I'll—"

He shook his fist.

It was vague in his mind, this plan. But then he had never been very good at planning things.

Death swept around a long curve in the river with the banks already dim, gray with early evening and the continuing rain. There were many good camping places along here, Shed thought. But they could go on a little farther . . . get that last bad spot behind them.

It was a little later when they saw the danger.

They were going along in the gloom, quiet, and Faith gasped.

Looking at her, and then ahead, Shed saw an unmistakable yellow glow through the brush on the bank.

Campfire.

Tingling, Shed immediately saw what else there was to see: a big wood boat, not much different from *Death*, dragged up on the clay bank, a length of rope stretched out between two trees and men's clothes hanging, smoke pluming up thickly black against the woods where the fire was.

"Hush!" Shed hissed. "No more making noise, now!"

Faith stared at him, frightened.

"We'll just go on by," Shed told her.

He hunkered down in the back of the boat, using the oar as tiller. The current was very fast, and he knew they would be past this spot, and around the far bend, inside two or three minutes. He kept his eyes riveted on the bank. No one must see them. *Anyone* meant trouble. He looked at his rifle in the bottom of the boat and wondered, despite all his precautions with it, whether there was any hope whatsoever that it would fire.

Quite suddenly, he was aware of all the physical stimuli around him that he had shut out for many hours: the soft plash of the boat's progress through the water, the drumming of the rain, the pockmarks on the surface, the soft hum of wind, a distant rumble of another bad place, the cold. Richard sat on the floor of the boat, patting his fat little hand in the water that sloshed around the bottom.

Shed hissed at him to stop, but of course Richard paid no attention.

Death moved on down the stream and came parallel with the campsite. Watching it with great intensity, Shed saw that the men had picked their spot well, protected from the raw wind by trees, in an area with plenty of firewood. He had not seen any of the men and didn't want to. In another minute the boat would be into the broad bend that would mean safety.

Out of the brush and trees near the beached boat, there was a sudden movement. A man, his features indistinguishable in the gloom of the shore, came into clear view.

He had not seen *Death* yet. He was casual, walking along as if looking for something on the bank. He was a tall man, and, Shed thought, young. Shed watched him intently, praying he would not look up—not see the boat. It was too far away to hear the whisper of water under the boat, and with any luck—

The man looked up. He stiffened, because he had looked up directly toward the boat. He straightened up and shaded his eyes although there was no sun.

His voice came clearly across the expanse of water: *"Hey!"*

Shed grabbed the oar and began paddling as hard as he could. "Don't pay him no mind. Don't answer. Pretend you don't hear nothing."

"Hey, there!" the voice called hoarsely. *"You in the boat!"*

Panic gave Shed new strength. Compared with all the other perils of this trip, the sound of a stranger's voice affected him like no other. Strangers could only mean trouble. He had to get away.

The bend was coming with what seemed agonizing slowness.

"You in the boat! Wait! Don't go down there!"

"Yeah," Shed grunted, fighting for breath. "Stay with you, huh? So you can rob our stuff? God-damned bastards."

There was a sharp, hollow report—a gunshot. Shed glanced back. Two more men had joined the first at the edge of the water. They were waving and yelling something, unintelligible with all the racket of bad place coming from somewhere beyond the bend. One of the men had what looked like a scatter-gun, and had fired it into the air. As Shed looked back, the man fired the other barrel against the sky.

"Crazy fool," Shed muttered, oaring for all he was worth. "Think you can scare John Riley Shed—!"

"*Wait!*" a voice came from far back now, tattered and faint in the wind.

A grove of trees hung out into the swollen river. Shed guided the boat in close to them, and around them, putting land between himself and the campsite.

"They can't catch us," he told Faith and the boy. "They got to load. We're going right on. Another ten, fifteen miles. That's all. Then, when we camp, I can be ready—watch. They had their chance. We beat 'em."

"Who were they?" Faith asked huskily.

"Dunno," Shed said, resting on the oar. "But we beat 'em."

The current was carrying them along faster. He had not noticed this before, but now he did. Apprehensively, he glanced ahead, thinking that he might have overlooked something in his haste to get by the camp. But there was nothing to do about that, he told himself. Getting by other men took precedence over anything else.

He could not see anything ahead. The river twisted back upon itself again just ahead. But he could hear the rumble he had fleetingly noticed earlier, and it was much closer.

It might be that one more bad spot, he thought. He had remembered it as being farther down.

"Nothing to fret about," he said, as much to reassure himself as anyone else. "Dangerous, running onto them folks. But they won't catch us now."

Richard grinned at him and splashed in the water on the bottom.

Death began to vibrate, as she had other times when trouble was near.

Shed frowned and precariously stood up, trying to see around the next bend. But he could not. It didn't seem fair, he thought, for one thing to pile right on top of another. After getting past other men, it looked like you ought to get some rest.

But *Death* was trembling, and moving faster through the water. The vibration frightened Shed a little, because already he could tell it was deepening, becoming almost a supernatural growl. The banks, choked with trees and fallen rock, had begun to move in. The river was coming to a curve and a narrows. The rain had almost stopped, so there was nothing to mask the roar coming ever closer.

Shed dug the oar in hard, staying to the center of the flow.

The river carried the boat out into the next bend and hurled it beyond.

He got a glimpse of what was ahead. His soul shriveled.

ELEVEN

It was much worse than anything before. As the boat raced toward it Shed thought, *I dreamed this.* But there was no time to know what this meant.

The gorge narrowed sharply ahead, and a great section of sheer rock wall had fallen. Chunks of stone of enormous size jutted from exploding water. Spray obscured all view of how far the bad place extended. The river swirled and beat back upon itself, writhing, hurling up gleaming clouds of spray that made an eerie, green-blue rainbow. There was no way around any of it, and no way, now, to stop. The roar was deafening and *Death* trembled from end to end, as if it had a life of its own, an instinct for its destruction.

"*Get down!*" Shed yelled. "*Under the seats! Hang on!*"

Faith obeyed instantly, perhaps thrown to the floor by the first ugly wave as it broke over the prow. Richard, well out of the reach of either her or Shed, looked up, frightened, but did not move beyond the buffeting he was taking.

"*Giddown!*" Shed howled again.

Too late. *Death* hurled into the spray. Shed was thrown sideways and lost the oar. His one good hand grasped the side rail as he clung for his life. He got another instant's look toward Richard, sitting on the floor as before, and Faith, bundled under the seat like a huddling animal.

There was an earsplitting crash and a tremendous jolt. Chunks of wood flew. The boat skewed sideways in boiling water, swamping. Through the brown, icy spray, Shed saw Richard lifted by the wave and tossed over the side, arms and legs spread wildly.

Richard hit the water and went under.

"*No!*" Shed screamed, but he couldn't hear his voice.

The boat slammed into another rock, submerged and went on over it. Another giant wave blinded Shed for an instant and the boat turned completely around, bolting through the hell with stunning speed, and then he caught sight of the rope that had held Richard. It was taut, going from the seat and over the side and into the water.

Richard was in the water, under the boat, being dragged.

The boat leaped into the air and came down sideways with a crash, throwing new water everywhere. Drenched, hysterical, Shed tried to fight his way to the center seat. He had to get to the rope. Nobody could live under the boat, the water holding him down, rocks bashing into him. But the boat leaped like an insane animal again, going around and around, and Shed was thrown back. He scrambled again, half blinded.

An enormous wall of rock shot past on the right. Then the boat dived head first into a deep, funnel-shaped pool. Shed had a moment of utter unreality, looking down across the length of the empty boat into the deeps of the turning pool. Then the boat smashed in, front first, and was hurled back up again on its side.

Shed got himself up out of the bottom. Somehow the

boat was still on top, half filled with water, being lifted up and thrown down again, hitting more submerged rocks. The sound was like express trains, the sound everywhere, killing him, and Richard was still under the boat somewhere, the water coming over the boat like frothing mountains, one after the other, battering.

Shed fought to reach the middle seat. Nothing else mattered. If the boat was going down, it was going down. If he was going to die, he was going to die. The rope—Richard—another incredible wave smashed him sideways and he tried to catch his weight on his hurt arm, and he felt bones grate, splintering, and the pain was a bright yellow wall that flashed through him, blanking all else out.

He managed to get back up. In the middle of the boat. He couldn't breathe and he tasted blood. He got a glimpse of his arm and saw bright red everywhere on it, the lower part dangling from a place where a jagged end of bone stuck out through the torn flesh. Then the boat went down and up and around again, hitting more things, the water going over him, some rocks flying by on both sides, and he saw everything through brown foam and bubbles, and he had to get to the rope.

He got the rope in his hand. He pulled on it. The weight was heavy. He could not get it to come up. Richard was still underneath. Sobbing, Shed hauled on the slippery rope and got some of it pulled in, and just then the boat turned around, more impacts, more breakage, and he was in deep water all around, the boat half sunk yet flying along through the rapids. He still had the rope. He hauled on it and caught sight of a heavy thing under the water, coming out to the side—arms and legs and clothing and hair—the golden hair aswirl in the water.

The boat leaped a small waterfall and Shed lost his hold on the rope. It sank deep again. The boat smashed over rocks all along the bottom, just underneath the surface. Shed could feel the dragging, bounding lurches of each hidden boulder, more water blinding him.

He wondered if it was ever going to end. He fought to haul the rope in again. He was screaming now. He could not hear his words. There was no reason to any of it any more, just the careening motion, the battering of rocks and blind sickness of the speed, carrying them on, down. There was a long slide down—*up!*—and then down again, making the boat fall entirely out from under him so that he fell sickeningly free for a split second, then crashed into the bottom of the boat again, and waves dashed over him, turning him. He had the rope but he couldn't pull it in. The river threw him up and down and up again, like sliding down a mountain in the snow, turning around constantly, hitting more things. He was still screaming, trying. It had been so long. He didn't know how long it had been. Everything was a blaze of pain and confusion and anguish. The rope was his only chance, all that mattered.

Then the river seemed suddenly to spit the boat forward, and it hurled itself through a last explosion of spray and out into calmer water. The walls—receding fast as the river widened again—became visible. The boat was half swamped, boards broken out of the sides, and blood pumped from Shed's arm, but none of that mattered, the rope was what mattered.

Shed hauled the rope up and, sobbing, managed to

catch something of Richard's clothing. Wet and cold, loose. He pulled, slipped, got a better grip and hauled Richard, very heavy and mud-cloaked and limp, out of the river and over the side of the boat.

Richard hit the water-filled bottom with a grotesque, sprawling looseness.

Shed turned and gauged the distance to shore. With no paddle they were being propelled along the middle. He clawed at the rope that attached Richard to the boat. The rope finally came free. Shed grabbed Richard's shirt front and went over the side, into the water, with him, capsizing the boat. He had to get to shore.

He went under, but not deep, hanging onto the boy. His natural buoyancy brought him up and he flailed with his broken arm and started to go under again. Then his feet hit bottom—a rock. He lunged, dragging the boy's dead weight in the water. He felt bottom again and got his balance, chest-deep in the savage current, and managed two staggering steps toward shore.

The bank rose fast and he climbed out, coughing and choking. It was a narrow gravel shelf beneath a near-vertical cliff. There was some muddy brush. None of that mattered. Shed dumped Richard on the pebbles and rolled him over. The boy did not move. His neck was bent at a strange angle.

Behind him, over the roar, Shed faintly heard Faith's cry.

He turned, electrified. He had forgotten. He did not know how this was possible, but he had forgotten her for an instant. It had been the boy—knowing he was being dragged, torn to pieces—the only kid you had ever really liked, one like *him,* his *bud*—that was why—

But there was no time to think, because Faith was in the water and the boat was going downstream and she was trying to fight the rush of water but it was taking her, too, and her head bobbed under, then came back, an arm waved, she vanished again.

"God damn you, Buttermilk!" Shed screamed, and plunged in.

He went over his head immediately. Then his feet found the jagged bottom, but the current knocked him sideways. He came up coughing and spitting, and Faith was right there beside him. Her arm flailed out for him. They touched. Shed caught her hand. The force of water against them both almost won out, but he managed to get his feet planted. He was in up to his neck—over her head—and almost beyond the ability to fight back. But the anger helped and he dragged her back a step, then another. A wave engulfed them but he got through it. The bank began to slope upward. Shed stumbled and fell heavily. He lost Faith's hand, but she stumbled into him, making her own way. He climbed out. She came behind him, sprawling onto the shale slope.

Driven, Shed crawled back to where he had put Richard down. The body had not moved. Shed threw an arm over him and hugged him to protect him from the Buttermilk.

"You're all right, boy," he said. "You're in good shape. Here you go. Wake up now. Here you go. Come on."

He pulled Richard to a sitting position and held his limp form with the fractured arm and pounded him on the back to try to get his breathing going again. Nothing happened. Richard's head lolled loosely. There was red froth on the side of his face. Shed tried not to see it.

Laying Richard out on his back, Shed worked first one of the boy's arms, then the other. He tried to do it like a pump. He had heard it helped. But that didn't do anything, so he knelt over the boy and put his mouth on his mouth and breathed in, hard, and then relaxed, and did it again. Some cold, muddy water discharged from Richard's mouth and nose.

"That's it," Shed said. "*That's* the boy! Belch that shit out, right? Good! Good! Come on, now!"

He breathed into Richard's mouth some more, then tried pushing in on his chest, to make the breathing start.

Faith lay where she had dropped on the water's edge, evidently too exhausted to raise her head. It was up to Shed alone, this battle, and he fought panic.

"You're all right, boy," he choked. "You *got* to be all right. God damn it, son you're like *me!* We're *alike!* You *got* to make it!"

He turned Richard over to pump on his back, but the boy's head rolled hideously, trying to turn all the way around, too. Shed fixed this.

"There you go," he sobbed. "*There* you go, now! That's it! Just let old John Riley Shed help you, right? You're all right! Sure you are! That's it! Just take it easy! I'll make you fine again! Nothing to worry about!"

Exhausted, he paused for a moment on his knees in the gravel and mud. He looked down at Richard's face. Richard's face was—

A spell came.

A small one.

Shed came back from it and was still kneeling there.

Nothing had changed except the sickness inside his brain.

He bent over and vomited, and brown water came up. It choked his nose, and when he wiped his good arm across his face, it came away all smeary red, from bleeding.

A large, warm splatter of water hit the back of Shed's neck. He looked up, and another drop hit his face. Rain was starting again.

Shed bent down and breathed into Richard's mouth some more. Then, after a while, he stopped and closed his eyes and knelt, slumped, feeling the rain.

Later, it was dark and the rain went away. Shed still knelt on the shelf beside the river, the distant boom of the rapids incessant, a backdrop to his own voice.

"You know what the trouble was?" he asked Richard, who still lay on the shelf beside him. "It wasn't all the river. I thought it was all the river. It was part the river. But it was part the boat, too.

"Awyep," Shed added, nodding. "The God-damned boat, boy. It wasn't no ordinary boat, you understand me? They named that boat *Death* for a reason. I think they did. Right. If we'd took *Mother*, think what a trip we might have had! I took the wrong boat. Then I got thinking it was all the river but it wasn't all the river, it was some the river, only not all. Part of it was the God-damned boat.

"Only, the boat's gone now. You don't need to fret. Aint' no boat, ain't no river. Not for us. Not no more. It ain't that far now to town. No, it ain't really. Some far, but not too far. Not for me. Not for us. We can walk it. We *can*."

Beside him, Faith moved, startling him. He turned and saw her crawl across the muddy little shelf, moving slowly, head down, eyes like great opals as they stared down at Richard where he lay.

Faith knelt over Richard, looked at him. Very tenderly, she pushed one last strand of hair back from his pale face. She touched the button on his shirt, and his lips, with her fingertips. Her face was full of wonderment and agony. The pain was so deep that she was beautiful.

Shed let her touch the tyke, because he knew she had a love for him, too. He wondered if she knew how much *he* loved Richard—that they were buds. He wanted to tell her this, but the words would not come.

Now the darkness was around them.

Faith looked up at Shed.

"You think we can't make it?" he said. "We can. I know how to git there from here. We ain't beat. Oh, won't be easy, not with this damned arm. Mess, ain't it? You ought to feel how it hurts. But I can still climb. I can get the tyke on my back and carry him just fine. I might be a worthless, ignorant old boy, but I'm hell for stout."

Faith said nothing. Her eyes were very strange.

"You got to help," Shed told her. "Make your own way behind me. But you can. Awyep. I know how strong you are. We'll just walk it on in. Take us long . . . twelve, maybe twenty hours. I dunno. But we can."

She stared at him.

He looked back at Richard, so peaceful in the dark. "You want to rest, boy? You tired? That's all right. That's fine. You want to sleep? Shucks, I know how that is. You just go right ahead. I can carry you anyways. I got one good arm left, right? Hey, you hear my joke—left and right, only it didn't mean left and right? Funny? Sure. Listen. You just take 'er easy. Nothing's going to hurt you now. I should of thought about the boat a long time ago. But I've thought about it now. We're safe, see? And we can walk it in from here. We're in good shape!"

He got to his feet. He was unsteady, and the pain made things blurry. He saw how hard the climb out of this place was going to be. It was going to be awful, but he must not let his family know that.

"I'll go first," he said. "I'll go up a little, stop and help you, right?" He nodded at Faith.

She stared at him.

"Sure," he grinned, and then he bent and picked Richard up, lifting him onto his shoulder. Richard rested there easily.

There was nothing to do but start. The boat was gone, the others were gone. But that was all just a vague memory already, because Shed had Faith and he had Richard and he had his mission: to get them to Eagle Grove.

"Don't you worry," he crooned, shrugging Richard into a more comfortable position on his shoulder. "We're good. We're fine. Ain't nothing else going to happen. I'm getting you there. Richard, you just sleep, that's the boy, you need your rest. Your momma is right behind us." He turned to Faith. "We'll go slow, climbing. You can use my legs to hang onto if you get short of holds. We'll go a little, rest a little."

"We can't," Faith said.

"We can, by God," Shed told her sternly, "because I said. Now here we go. Just take it easy, right? Good. That's it. Up we go. Everything is fine."

He started to climb.

TWELVE

"See? You see? I told you!"

The thin sunlight was warm on Shed's back, and he paused for a moment, triumphant, and waited for either the boy or the woman to say something even though they had been silent throughout yesterday's terrible hike and the long night of cold. He shrugged the boy into a slightly easier position on his shoulder and looked back at Faith, who trailed him by a few paces.

"We made it. Like I said."

The wide street of Eagle Grove lay before them. They were on the edge of the town. The sunlight glistened on mud pocked and torn by wagon wheels and animals, and the twin rows of board buildings looked pale and empty in the illumination of the morning.

"Find the doc," Shed told them. "You'll be all right then."

He started into the town, Richard in his grasp like a baby. It hurt to walk, because of a fall, and his left arm dangled, bone protruding from a tear in the flesh that had begun to turn greenish. The thing smelled, and this morning, on the last few miles' walk, it had almost made Shed sick. But they were here now and it would be all right.

A door opened on one of the small buildings as Shed

approached with his family. A man looked out, made a gasping noise, and hurriedly closed the door again. Up in the next block, some men working around a wagon pointed, and Shed could hear their excited, puzzled voices.

"News travels," he chuckled. "Awyep. Strangers comin'. Mountain man comin'. Look at 'em ahint that window there. See 'em stare! Don't matter. They won't bother us none."

He slogged on up the street. Of course he was lying, for the benefit of his family. He had never openly entered a town like this without meeting trouble, and so he had not done it for many years. There would be trouble, he thought vaguely. He wished he had not lost his gun. But that was over . . . you couldn't go back. He had to think about getting the boy and the woman fixed up now, and worry about everything else later.

"See up there in the next block?" he asked Richard. "Bigger buildings. Bank, probably. Lawyer. Post office. Doctor, too, I'll bet. Won't be no problem now. Git you to the doc, git you fixed up."

Some children stood on a boardwalk, watching. They looked frightened. Shed gave them his most ferocious glare and they silently moved back against the wall, trying to avoid the stare. A pudgy little man, his suspenders dangling down the sides of his trousers, hurried out of a house and came into the street to intercept Shed. The little man looked upset.

"My name is Greene," he said. "I'll help—" And he reached out as if to touch Richard.

"No!" Shed growled, and swung his arm like a club.

The little man jumped back, eyes wide with fear.

Shed walked on. It was hard to walk a straight line and he was not sure why. He was weak and confused, and yet a part of his mind was feverishly clear. He saw the men ahead of him, watching, and the faces behind the windows, and he knew the sensation he was creating. He was sure it was going to be bad. It was always bad around other people. There was always trouble. But he had come for the doctor and he was going to find the doctor and that was first.

He walked into the next block, so that now the town was closing in behind him. The feeling of pursuit was very, very strong. His vision was strangely blurry and he could not breathe right. He kept going.

"Nothing to worry about," he lied for Richard's benefit. "Your bud ain't going to let nothing happen. You just rest easy, that's a boy."

He spotted the small sign hanging under a porch roof with a name and the letters *M.D.* behind it. He had learned to recognize this symbol, and headed for it.

The office was in a row of shops. Shed limped up onto the porch and tested the office door. The handle turned. He shoved the door open and stood back to let Faith go in first, and then followed her.

The front room was like the parlor of a house, so dim after the sun that Shed was blind for a few moments. He smelled dust and medicines and felt the enclosure of the walls. Then he began to be able to make out some tables and chairs and a sofa and a lamp. It was the room where patients waited, Shed realized.

Faith went over to the sofa. It had lace fringe on it. She reached out a thin, trembling hand and touched the material as if it were a source of wonder.

A door opened from an inside room. A man came out. He was young. He looked agitated but he was trying not to show it. The pale light glinted off his thick glasses.

"Who are you?" he asked thickly. "What do you want?"

It seemed a singularly stupid question to Shed. He shrugged Richard, on his shoulder. "Boy's hurt. Woman's hurt too, maybe."

The doctor stared from Richard and Shed to Faith. "My God. Where did you come from?"

"Fix the boy!" Shed said, anger swelling his voice.

The doctor's face worked. "Bring them both–bring them in here." He pointed to the interior door.

Shed nodded to Faith, and she went in first. Shed followed.

The second room was the working office. It was arranged to the side of the waiting room, so that a wing of it looked onto the street through sun-bright curtains. It had a bench on one side, a desk, some cabinets with bottles and instruments in them, and a narrow bed against the wall. It was a good room, like a bear's den but different.

"Sit right there," the doctor said to Faith, pointing to the bed. He turned back to Shed. "Put him there. On the bench."

Shed gently put Richard down. Richard's head bumped.

The doctor said something secret to Faith. She did not respond. Shed waited. The doctor looked at him and then walked over and looked down at Richard.

"He's asleep," Shed told him.

The doctor raised his face to Shed's, his expression a mixture of horror and fear that was obscured because his eyes were not visible behind the sun-glared glasses. "My God, man—!"

"Name of Shed. Come down from the mountains." It was a grave struggle now to make sense, because for some reason he wanted to cry. It made his voice shake. "Family of us. Her, this 'un, his bud, his sis. God-damned Buttermilk got the little girl, other little boy. Almost got us." His mind turned off for a moment and then came back. He had been distracted by moving shadows on the porch, beyond the curtains. People out there. Gathering. Why?

"Let me start on that arm of yours," the doctor said grimly.

Shed backed off. "No! Take care of him first!"

The doctor stared at him.

"He's my bud!" Shed explained.

The doctor said nothing. There was a new sound in the room. Faith was weeping. It was a long, steady sound, as if much was coming out.

"You're a doc," Shed said. "You can fix him. *I* couldn't, but I'm ignorant. You can do it."

"Man—" the doctor said thickly. "I'm . . . *sorry*."

The truth nudged ponderously and tried to get in. "He ain't . . . asleep?"

The doctor shook his head.

"I brang him overland. Him and her. River took the rest. Busted our boat. But I was smart and I had a rope on him so I got him out, and then I dragged her back out, too. Then we clumb, and walked. Might have been here last night only I fell down a hill and then I got mixed up where we was for a while."

The doctor moved forward. "I'll look at your arm."

Shed pulled back convulsively. "No! Look at *him!*"

"I told you—"

"What are *they* doing out there?" Shed demanded, pointing at all the moving shadows on the curtains.

"I don't know. But I'll look at your arm, and then—"

"No, God damn it, no! You're a doctor, ain't you? Doctors fix things. Fix this boy, then! You think I can't pay? Is that it? I can pay. I can have so many pelts in this room inside a couple months, you won't be able to move around in it. —Fix him up!"

"It's too late."

Shed looked at the doctor. "But you can fix him."

"No."

"He . . . ain't asleep?"

"No. I'm sorry."

Tears stung Shed's eyes. He heard a moan, and then realized that the sound had come from him. The shadows moved on the curtains.

Shed turned to Faith. "You could of told me. You knew. You didn't say nothing. I know what you think of me. You didn't have to do this, though. That wasn't right."

She looked up at him and she was still crying too.

The doctor grasped his good arm. "Sit down here, man."

"*No,* God damn it! *No,* God damn it! *No!*" Shed pulled away and strode to the window. He peered out through the lace. There were five men. They had guns—rifles and shotguns. They stood at the foot of the steps, grimly talking among themselves in low, close-guarded tones. Across the street was a scattering of onlookers.

"Yeah," Shed said bitterly. "Don't matter about my bud

or nothing else. Just make sure they git *me* . . . earn theirselfs their bounty money."

"We don't have law in this town right now," the doctor said. "Those men are strangers. Our marshal died a few weeks ago and those men aren't law. They came down the river. Don't know how they ever made it."

"They want me. They all want me."

"Who are you?"

"It don't matter," Shed said, making his decision. "I need a gun."

"I don't have a—"

Shed sprang across the room and savagely knocked the doctor back against the wall. The doctor's glasses spun in the air and hit the floor.

"I said," Shed grated, "I want—"

"In the desk, the bottom drawer! But it's—"

Shed jerked the desk drawer open. Under some papers was the gun. It was a very old revolver. The trigger was loose. He could not understand if this was a joke or what.

"It's broken," the doctor said. "I tried to tell you. I never had it fixed after it broke. There's no need—"

"Will it fire?"

"No, and even if it would, there are no bullets; I threw them away—"

Shed nodded. "All right. It don't matter." He shoved the gun in the front of his belt.

"Sit down here," the doctor pleaded, putting his glasses back on his nose. "You're a sick man."

There was a tap on the outside office door.

"They want me," Shed said.

"Maybe not. I'll go see. It might be a patient."

A male voice outside called: *"Shed? We need to talk to you."*

Shed smiled at the doctor. "Ain't no patient."

"There's a back door," the doctor said hoarsely.

"With this arm? Busted up in my chest? —No, an' there'd be people out back, too. Count on it."

"What are you going to do?"

Shed drew in a deep breath. He walked over to where Faith sat, head down, still weeping softly. "I know what you think of me," he said. "I know what I done to you and what you think. Then I let the Buttermilk have the other tykes. I talked big, but I messed up. But I got you here, you and him. And even if all the rest was—" He stopped because his voice broke.

He turned and walked back to where Richard lay on the bench. Richard did not look quite the same now and Shed was embarrassed because grown men did not cry. You took what you got, that was all there was to it.

"God-damned Buttermilk," Shed breathed.

He turned to the doctor. "He was my bud."

The doctor looked puzzled, afraid.

Shed explained, "We was the same."

The doctor didn't say anything.

"Shed?" the voice outside called again. *"We want to talk!"*

"Awyep," Shed breathed, and had to smile at how dumb people were, sometimes.

"I can help you," the doctor said. "Let me try."

Shed ignored him. He looked down at Richard again. It had all been about Richard, he saw now. "Ah, damn it," he whispered to Richard, "you and me, right?"

Richard lay very still.

Shed bent over and kissed the boy on the mouth. The lips were cold and firm. Shed did not want to stop kissing him because he had never kissed anybody like this: because he loved them. He had the crazy thought that maybe Richard could draw the life out of him and take it into his own body and be all right again, and for an instant the kiss felt as if Shed's own life really was being sucked out of him. But then the feeling passed and he stopped right away.

He started for the inner office door. "Guess you'll like this," he told Faith.

"Wait!" the doctor said.

"Take care of them," Shed said. "They're good people."

"Wait! You can't walk out there like that!"

Shed went into the outer office. He drew the useless gun and he moved. He reached for the front doorknob.

"If you go out there with that gun in your hand, they'll think—!"

Shed opened the door with the heel of his hand. He paused for an instant and then went out.

They were standing at the foot of the steps. They all looked up, startled. They jumped when they saw the gun. Shed yelled something and pointed the gun at one of them. It was all as he expected, because they reacted swiftly and well. He saw and heard and felt the explosions all at the same time. Things exploded and tore apart all through him and he hit the wooden wall and then more things hit and it was like a little spell had come.

Then he was wet and cold, because he had fallen off the porch—he was at the foot of the steps in the mud and the sun hurt his eyes and there were people over him close and people over him far. One of the faces was the doctor. One, Shed recognized with soft shock, was Faith. The other men stood back.

A voice said, "I don't get it! I don't get it! We just wanted to ask him if he could help us!"

"That's Shed, ain't it?" another voice asked hoarsely. "We been looking for him. My brother went up in that country last fall, he didn't come out, we thought somebody like Shed could tell us something—maybe help us hunt—"

The boy who had the new rifle. Shed realized, distantly, that this must be the one they sought. He was struck by a sense of enormous irony. They hadn't wanted him at all. Not in the way he had thought. Not in the way they had thought. But things were moving away swiftly now, so this did not matter, either.

Faith's face was large in his vision. Her tears hit his face as they fell. They were warm.

"Don't matter," he told her, and smiled.

"It does," she said fiercely. "It does! It *does!*"

He looked at her, aware of things the doctor was trying to do. But he was very surprised by her voice and feeling. It dawned upon him that now she was crying *for him.*

"It does?" he whispered, awed.

"Richard loved you, don't you know that? You were the only one, the *only* one, who ever tried with him, talked with him—and you tried so hard—"

Ah, God. She was right. He had tried hard. But it had never much occurred to him, before this moment, that you ever got anything for the trying. There had been so few results in his life. But now she was crying. That was a result. Richard had loved him, she said. *Him.* That was a result.

He thought she was still talking to him. He could not be sure. His hearing was gone, and his vision was retreating. But so was the pain, and in its place was a very great astonishment and joy.